MAX'S MISSION

WAGNER BRIGADE

BOOK SIX

ASHLEY A QUINN

TCA PUBLISHING LLC

ISBN: 978-1-959943-30-3

PROLOGUE

*F**ourteen months ago...*

Acid burned in Tad Gaultier's esophagus, and he swallowed hard, attempting to force it back where it belonged. His hands shook as he set the manila envelope on the counter.

He didn't want to do this.

But there wasn't any other way. Not if he wanted to keep his family safe.

He'd screwed up.

Royally.

Margot would be okay, though. She was the toughest person he knew. She'd navigate Em and Lily through this, and they'd come out the other side just fine. And much better off than they would if he stayed.

He stepped away from the counter. It took a monumental effort—like ripping off a limb—but he tore his gaze away from the envelope and turned. Leaning down, he picked up his duffel and raised the handle on his suitcase.

The wheels rumbled on the floor as he headed for the front door. Cool metal teased his skin as he turned the doorknob.

With one final glance over his shoulder, he said a silent goodbye and walked outside to a waiting vehicle and the federal agent in the driver's seat.

ONE

P*resent day...*

It took everything Margot Gaultier had not to drop to her office floor in a heap. Her hands shook, and she clenched the phone to her ear to stop the tremors. She rolled her lips inward, bringing a halt to their quivering.

One of her daughters squealed and waved her toy, showing off the "You did it!" message, telling her she'd matched all the shapes correctly.

Margot forced a smile, then turned so Emily couldn't see her face. The little girl didn't need to see her mother on the verge of a breakdown.

"I know this is a shock, but the sooner you can come, the better." The detective kept his voice soft and polite. Margot wanted to reach through the phone and shake him and ask him why his world wasn't tipped upside down too.

Instead, she forced herself to be civil. "I understand," she replied quietly. "It'll take me a day or so to get there."

"If you could keep me informed of your plans, that would be great. I want to stay available for when you arrive. Hopefully, we can make this process as quick and painless as possible."

"I'd like that too." She closed her eyes, blinking back the moisture gathering there.

"All right. I'll see you soon, Mrs. Gaultier. I'm so sorry for your loss."

Margot wanted to scoff, but held back. She'd suffered the loss a long time ago, just in a different way. "Thank you. Goodbye." She hung up and squeezed her eyes shut. A single tear slid free. She swiftly wiped it away before the girls could see.

Emily squealed again, closer this time. A moment later, Margot felt a tug on her pant leg. She glanced down, forcing a smile for her daughter's benefit. "Did you match them again?"

"I matched. All by myself!" Emily held the toy up.

"I see. Good job, sweetie. Do you want to try again?"

The little girl bobbed her head and sank to her butt, engrossed in her toy.

Margot inhaled a steadying breath. She needed a moment.

"Sweetie, you stay here with your sister." Margot pushed back from the desk. "Mommy will be right back."

Emily didn't even look up. Margot glanced at Lily, who sat beside the desk with a box of giant crayons and a coloring book. Both girls were content for the moment.

Getting up and crossing the small room, Margot left her office, closing the door behind her, and went next door to Annabeth's office. She was thankful they were still in the building phase of their little clinic. Focusing on patient care would be nigh on impossible after that bombshell.

She rapped her knuckles on the wood as she stepped into the doorway. "Hey, do you have a minute?"

The smile of greeting on her friend's face swiftly died

when she took in Margot's expression. "What's wrong? Sit. Where are the girls?"

"They're next door. I—" The sudden lump in her throat cut off her words. She sank into the guest chair as she swallowed hard and tried again. "A detective just called. From North Dakota. Tad's dead." She'd never expected to see her ex-husband again after the way he left, but knowing it was now a certainty brought out all the emotions she'd buried fourteen months ago.

"What?" Annabeth breathed, her eyes growing round. "What happened? And what was he doing in North Dakota?"

"They're not one hundred percent certain it's him, but they found a set of keys on a body that matched an abandoned vehicle." She glanced down, picking at her hands. "Something in the car gave them a name, I guess. The—the detective asked if I could come up and help them identify the body. I guess they're not sure it's him."

"Oh my God." Annabeth stared at her with wide eyes. "I'm assuming they found his driver's license online, if they knew to call you. How are you supposed to ID him if they can't tell it's him from his license?"

"The detective wants me to look at the personal effects. He said there was a car key in his pocket that goes to a car they found months ago, abandoned. The vehicle was full of stuff. Like he'd been living in it. He also asked me to submit a DNA sample from the girls." She dropped her head into her hands. "Oh, God, Annabeth. I don't want to do this."

Annabeth got up, moving around to sit next to her. She laid a hand on Margot's shoulder. "I'm so sorry, Margot. What do you need from me? I can go with you. Or Dean can. We both could, if you want."

"Um..." Margot threaded her hands together and stared at them. Her mind swirled with a million thoughts, but one thought screamed louder than the others. She didn't want to take the girls with her. "Actually, could you and Dean watch the girls while I'm gone? Traveling with them is a nightmare, and they don't need to be exposed to the situation."

"Of course we can watch them. But you're not going up there by yourself, are you?"

Margot shrugged. She hadn't had time to figure out what she was doing.

"Take someone with you. Max would go, I'm sure."

A pair of lovely, silvery blue eyes popped into her mind. She knew Annabeth was right; he'd help her in a heartbeat. But he already did so much for her and the girls, she didn't want to impose more. That was the very reason she had the girls with her today after her sitter called and said she was sick. She'd become too reliant on Max and wanted to break the cycle. He wasn't her husband or her significant other. It wasn't his job to rescue her all the time. She was grateful he was her friend, but she didn't want him to think she only hung around for what he could do for her. She liked him for so many more reasons than that.

"Don't." Annabeth aimed a finger at Margot's face.

Margot frowned. "Don't what?"

"Don't take the choice away from him. I know you think you're imposing, but Max would do anything for you. Let him help. You shouldn't do this alone. No one should."

A bang and a screech from next door propelled Margot to her feet. "I'll think about it." And she would, but she'd never ask him to go. It was one thing to ask him to babysit or to come fix something at her house. Flying to North Dakota on short notice to confirm her ex-husband was dead was on a whole other level.

"Let me know when you need us," Annabeth called.

Margot gave her a thumbs up as she hurried out of the office. After she rescued her daughters from each other, she had a lot to think about.

Two

The deep-throated purr of Max's car engine cut abruptly as he shut the vehicle off in Margot's driveway, Annabeth's cryptic message still fresh in his mind.

Margot could use a distraction.

Like, what the hell did that mean? Were the girls extra ornery today? Had something happened? When he replied to ask why, she ghosted him.

So, here he was with a carton of Margot's favorite pineapple passionfruit gelato, hoping she wouldn't be pissed that he'd shown up unannounced when she'd had a rough day.

Pebbled gravel crunched under his flip-flops as he walked up the short path to her front door. The little pale-yellow bungalow with its pink front door could fit inside his living room, but Margot insisted it was fine for her and the twins. He and the others had tried to convince her the other house she looked at closer to his would be a better fit and give her and the girls more room, but she wouldn't be swayed. The neighborhood was nice, and she could literally step out her back door and yell for Annabeth, which, Max was sure, had been the deciding factor. He couldn't blame her for wanting to be near her friend. She'd moved thousands of miles from home to a foreign country after a major life change. It was probably comforting to have her best friend close by.

Through the wooden front door, he could hear Emily screeching. One side of his mouth lifted. That girl was hardly ever quiet. Usually only when she was asleep.

Raising a fist, he knocked on the door.

Thirty seconds passed with no answer, so he tried again. "Margot?"

When another thirty seconds went past and she still hadn't answered, he tried the door. It was unlocked.

Pushing the colorful door inward, he stepped inside. "Margot? It's Max." The small living room he walked into was empty, though it looked like a tornado tore through it. From the short hallway to the left, he heard splashing and Emily's shriek of joy. A moment later, Lily joined in. Now he understood why she hadn't answered. It was bath time.

With a few strides, he crossed the living room and rounded the corner to the hallway, looking right into the bathroom. Margot sat on her knees on the floor, water splotches all over her clothes. As he watched, she scooped a cup of water out of the bath and dumped it over Lily's soapy head.

"Margot."

She yelped and spun around. "Jesus!" She pressed a hand to her chest. "Max!" Closing her eyes for a moment, she inhaled a breath through her nose. "You scared me. I didn't hear you."

"I noticed. The door was open, so I let myself in. Need a hand?"

She spared a quick glance at the girls, who were busy pushing plastic fish through the water at each other. Em looked up and saw him. With a wide smile, she lifted her fish out of the water to show him, spraying her mother with soapsuds in the process.

Margot closed her eyes for a second and sighed. "Um... no. I think we're about done. What are you doing here?"

He held up the gelato carton. "Annabeth said you needed a distraction. Pineapple passionfruit gelato fixes everything."

Margot looked away, a hardness settling over her face that confused him. "I'll just bet she did," she mumbled.

"What?" He frowned.

"Nothing." She waved a hand, looking at him again. The smile she sent his way didn't reach her eyes. "As much as that sounds wonderful, I need to get these heathens to bed. I'm sorry you came all the way over here for nothing."

Max narrowed his eyes, sure now more than ever that something was wrong, and Annabeth was right to send him over. "I didn't. Put them to bed. The gelato—and I—will be waiting for you when you're done."

"Max—"

He ticked a finger. "No arguments. I don't know what you need a distraction from, but Annabeth was right that you do. I'll be out there when you're done." He tipped his head toward the kitchen and living room as he stepped back.

"I'm fine, really."

"Then we can enjoy our gelato and some light conversation before you go to bed."

She stared at him for a beat. "Anyone ever tell you you're pushy?"

"All the time, babe. All the time." Grinning, he faded into the hall and walked away before she could truly kick him out.

Entering the kitchen, he took one look at the sink full of dirty dishes and the mess on the island and put the gelato in the freezer. It could wait.

No wonder she hadn't wanted to relax after the girls were in bed. She couldn't.

He found a dish rag in a drawer and a clean sponge and set to work. Squirting dish soap in the sink, he turned on the faucet. While he waited for the sink to fill with hot, soapy water, he scraped the last bits of food from the girls' plates into the trash, then did the same with the skillet. All of it went into the pile of dirty dishes on the other side of the sink.

When the sink was full, he shut the water off, then cleaned the small island Margot used as a table. Once it was clean, he wiped out the girls' booster seats, then set about washing the dishes. He had them all done and in the drying rack by the time Margot emerged from the hallway. He'd also picked up the toys scattered around the living room and put the crayons back in their box, stowing them on a shelf with the coloring books.

Her reaction to him cleaning up was not what he expected, though. He'd thought she'd be surprised and thank him, or, considering her attitude in the bathroom, get a little defensive that he'd taken the chore off her plate.

Instead, she burst into tears.

Eyes wide and feeling more confused than ever, he crossed to her side. "Margot. Hey, honey, what's wrong?" He put a gentle hand around her bicep and tugged, pulling her into his chest. When she didn't back away, he wrapped his arms around her and stroked the back of her head. The silky blonde hair under his fingers was cool to the touch and just slightly damp.

She clutched the sides of his shirt and buried her face in his neck. With a hiccup, she looked up. "I'm sorry. I'm—" Another sob choked off her words. She inhaled a breath, making a snort-snuffle sound.

Max took her hand and led her over to the couch, handing her some tissues from the box on the end table. "Take a breath. Tell me what's wrong."

She took the tissues and dabbed at her face. "Nothing."

"That's crap, and you know it. Tell me what's going on. Why did Annabeth say you need a distraction?"

"Annabeth has a big mouth." She sniffed and wiped her face again.

"She's worried about you."

Margot sighed. "I know."

"So, what's going on? Why are you so upset?"

"I'm not."

He snorted. "The tear tracks on your face tell me otherwise."

"I'm not upset. Just... overwhelmed."

"Because of the girls? What did Em do today?" That girl could try the Pope's patience.

She barked a short laugh. "It wasn't Emily."

"No?"

"No." She reached over him for more tissues, then blew her nose. When she finished, she stared at the wad of white in her hand.

He lightly touched her forearm, trying to gain her attention. "So, should I keep guessing?"

Margot lifted her head. The bleakness in her eyes punched him in the gut. He hadn't seen that look since he'd first met her when her life was in total turmoil.

"I got a phone call today. From a detective in North Dakota." She rolled her lips in for a moment, then let them go on a slow exhale. "My ex-husband is dead."

Shock made him sit up straighter. He stared for several seconds, a frown forming as he mulled her words over. "You said a detective called? Not the medical examiner's office?"

"Yeah. I don't know many details. He didn't seem like he wanted to discuss it too much over the phone. Apparently, um..." She trailed off and rubbed at her temple. "Um, he was... decomposed, so they're not completely certain it's him."

Max's eyes narrowed. "How did they know to call you, then? *Why* did they call you? You're divorced."

"They found keys in his clothing that went to a car they'd

found abandoned months ago. I guess something in it gave them his name." She paused, tucking a lock of hair behind her ear. "The girls are his next-of-kin, which makes me his next-of-kin since they're so young. He doesn't have any other family except for a few distant cousins. The detective asked if I could submit a DNA sample from one of the twins. Dental records weren't an option. He—" She stopped, swallowing hard. "He was missing quite a few teeth, he said." Her gaze dipped, then she turned her head away.

His inner radar went off. It was something about the way her gaze darted off. He set a hand over hers, squeezing. "There's more, isn't there?"

Her eyes met his, then she looked away again, pulling her hand out from under his. "Stop reading me."

"It's not like I really have to try, Margot. Your face is an open book. What else does the detective want?"

She sighed and muttered a soft curse under her breath before she met his gaze again, piqued. "He wants me to come up there and identify him from the things they found in his car. He's got questions too."

Like a lightbulb illuminating the darkness, Annabeth's reasons for sending him over became crystal clear.

Max nodded. His fingers itched to reach out and touch her again, but he didn't want to push things. "You plan to go alone, don't you?"

"I don't have anyone else." Margot shifted in her seat, looking over her shoulder toward the hallway where the girls slept. "Annabeth and Dean are watching the girls. I'm an only child to two elderly parents who didn't really want to be parents. I'm not even sure where they are right now."

Max's eyebrows met his hairline. "You realize you have a town full of people who would hop on a plane with you in a heartbeat, right? Any of us would drop everything and go with you. All you have to do is ask."

She pushed to her feet and stormed into the kitchen, throwing open the freezer to get to the gelato.

He got up and followed her. "Margot."

She aimed a glare at him as she yanked open a drawer and withdrew an ice cream scoop.

He stayed by the island, not wanting to crowd her. Why she was so angry, he didn't understand. Her attitude didn't put him off their discussion, though. If anything, he wanted to know more—wanted to understand why she was so surly. And somehow, he had to get her to see that she wasn't a burden but part of their small, ragtag family.

She heaped gelato into two bowls, tapping the scoop on the side with a little more force than necessary. "I know I'm being unreasonable, but—" She flattened her lips, glancing away. When she met his gaze again, moisture shimmered there.

With a sniff, she grabbed a spoon, jabbing it into her gelato. "First, I'm not used to having help. Before Tad, I did everything alone. It's the curse of having parents who were in their forties when I was born and didn't really want me. They left me alone. A lot. Even when they were home, I had a nanny." She swirled the gelato in her bowl, staring at it. Deep furrows etched her brow. "Second, you all have done so much for me already. What happened with Tad—it's my mess."

Hoping to diffuse some of the frustration and anger he saw brewing in her eyes, Max inched closer, trying to offer her a shoulder to lean on without actually touching her. "Okay, I understand the alone thing. But how is this stuff with Tad your mess? The man left you with no notice." He didn't know much about what happened with her ex. She never talked about him, but he knew that much.

"Something drove him away." She jabbed the spoon into the gelato again, then gave the bowl a soft shove before bracing her hands on the edge of the counter. "Whether it was my drive to succeed or becoming parents unexpectedly—I'm not completely blameless."

Max closed the distance in one quick step. He'd heard enough. Grasping her chin, he tipped her face, forcing her to look him in the eye. "He left you. No discussion, no expressing his concerns. He just up and left. Whether he didn't like something about you or the life you two had, it's not your fault."

Margot opened her mouth to say something, but he shifted his hand, cupping her jaw and slipping his thumb over her lips. "You are not the problem. He is. Nor are you a burden to people."

He could feel her jaw flex beneath his hand as she held his gaze. After a moment, she shook her head, her eyes telling him she wanted to refute his words.

He soldiered on before she could. "And as far as helping you goes, that's what friends do. Especially our group of friends. We're more than that. We're a family." Max's heart thumped at the swirling emotions that blazed through her blue eyes. They moved too quickly for him to discern what she was thinking, though.

After a beat, she stepped out of his hold. "But I'm not. Not really. I'm just Annabeth's tagalong."

Max forced his hands to stay at his sides. He wanted to grab her and shake some sense into her; at the same time, he wanted to hold her close. This was a side of Margot he'd never seen. She was an unsure, almost scared woman waiting to be hurt.

In all the time he'd known her, she'd been on the quieter side—except around her daughters and Annabeth—and it suddenly made sense why. She felt like she was on the outside looking in.

The realization overrode the part of his brain that cautioned him to go slow and to give her space. He laid his hand over one of hers. "No, Margot, you're not. The moment Dean brought you into the fold, you were part of the family. You and the girls."

This was not a subject he was willing to debate, so he changed the subject. "Now, have you booked a flight north yet?"

She pulled her hand away again and snatched her bowl off the counter, cradling it against her chest. Picking up the spoon, she waved it at him. "I know what you're doing, Max. Changing the subject won't magically make things different."

Stepping back and giving her some space, he picked up his bowl and spoon, fighting a frown. "No, but maybe by doing so, eventually you'll come to realize I'm right. Now answer my question."

She stabbed her gelato again. "No."

He arched an eyebrow. "No, you won't answer my question or no, you haven't booked a flight?"

"No, I haven't booked a flight."

His lips stretched in a smile. "Good. I'll get on that and book us on one. When do you want to leave?"

"Max..." she ground out through clenched teeth. If he'd been frozen, like their gelato, the fire in her eyes would have melted him.

He pointed his spoon at her before taking a quick bite. "Don't argue with me. Not on this." He softened his voice a bit. He didn't want to push her too far. Yet. "You need someone with you. I'll follow your lead, but I know we'd all be happier if you didn't go alone. You don't know what you're walking into or what the cops are thinking. Let me be the shoulder to prop you up, to have your back? Please?"

She stuffed a spoonful of gelato into her mouth and looked away, the angry frown on her face turning slightly less belligerent and more thoughtful. Finally, she looked at him again. "This is hard for me. Accepting help. Annabeth badgered me into moving in with her when Tad left; otherwise, I'd still be in Texas, struggling while I spent ninety hours a week at the hospital and the rest trying not to be a stranger to my children."

The vulnerability in her eyes cut deep into Max's heart.

"She's the only person—other than Tad—I've ever truly trusted, and I need her now to watch my kids while I straighten this out." She swirled her spoon through her treat once more. "But you're right. I don't want to go alone. I'm dreading going at all."

"So, does that mean you won't protest if I tag along?" he asked when she paused.

Margot scooped up another bite of gelato, slipping it past her lips. She glanced away, a deep furrow forming between her eyes, and sighed. "I suppose not." She pinned him with a narrow-eyed look. "But that doesn't mean I'll let you buy my ticket."

Max shoved a bite of his own gelato into his mouth, hiding a smirk. One way or another, he'd get his way. "How about you let me arrange all the travel? You can pay me back."

She snorted. "No. I know you. We'll end up in first class, which I can't afford."

He turned up the wattage on his smile, hoping to persuade her to see his side of things. "But I can. For both of us. How about this? I get the first-class seats, but you pay me for the cost of an economy ticket?"

Her frown returned. She opened her mouth to speak, but he raised a hand, cutting her off. "I don't want to sit in economy for a flight that long. I'm too tall, and I can afford not to be smushed. I also don't want you to sit alone. That's just dumb."

Which was true, but if she pushed back too hard, he'd suck it up so she didn't have to sit by herself. He hoped she didn't, though. They would both be much more comfortable in first class. "And it's not like an extra first-class ticket will break me. I'm not Brooke rich, but you know I'm far from poor."

She pursed her lips and blinked at him. Finally, her expression relaxed. "All right, fine. You win. But can we not stay in a super fancy hotel? The local Holiday Inn is fine."

"I will see what they have there." And if the local budget hotels were all booked up, he'd not shed a tear if they had to stay at a fancier place.

THREE

"Okay, so you saw the pack of diapers I put in the bedroom? And Max brought in the groceries." Margot glanced toward Annabeth's kitchen, mentally checking off all the things on her list so she could leave the girls without worrying... Much.

She bit her lip, looking at the pile of food she and Annabeth were working to put away. "Do you think that's enough milk? Maybe I should go grab another gallon." She'd spent the entire day packing yesterday, and it still didn't feel like enough. At two-and-a-half, the twins' appetites and energy levels were unpredictable. How much clothing and food the girls went through depended on what they did that day. Sometimes even on how much they slept.

Annabeth grabbed Margot's biceps and leaned in. "Relax. If it's not here or there's not enough, we can get it. The store is down the road, and your house is literally yards away. We'll be fine."

"I know, it's just—" Margot stopped and sighed. She glanced at Lily, who sat on the floor with Dean, putting a puzzle together. Emily had a light up toy on her lap and was going to town, punching buttons. Logically, she knew they'd be fine. But she'd never left them for more than twelve hours before, and she'd always been in the same city. This time, she'd be in an entirely different country.

"I get it, Margot. I know you're worried, but they'll be fine." Annabeth gave her a slight shake, then let go. "Quit worrying. Please?"

Margot blew out a breath, ruffling the hair around her face. "I'll try." And she would, but she knew it would stay in the back of her mind and niggle at her the entire time she was gone.

Annabeth looked toward the living room, where Max crouched near Emily, watching her play. "Go get him and get out of here. Is Ezra picking you up, or are you meeting him at the airport?"

"He's probably at my house, waiting. It made more sense for him to drive us all there and leave his car than for him and Max to drive there." Ezra was going to take them to San José, where they would catch a commercial flight to the United States.

"That sounds like a good plan. Are you ready for the frigid temperatures that will greet you?"

"Ugh, no. I think only Alaska would be worse this time of year." She was a warm weather girl. Having grown up in California, she'd stayed in the warm weather states throughout college and med school deliberately. She didn't even like to ski, much to her parents' consternation. It had been one of the few activities they'd attempted to include her in. She was decent at it, but she just couldn't get over the cold that went with it. She hated it.

Annabeth chuckled. "Probably. But hopefully, it'll be quick."

"Yeah." She'd been crossing her fingers for that very thing

since the detective called, but deep down, she had a feeling it would be much longer and more complicated.

Pushing away from the counter, she walked toward her daughters. "Give Mommy a hug, girls. I have to go."

Emily tossed her toy to the side and got up from the floor, running over to Margot. Crouching, Margot caught the girl and inhaled her fresh, little girl scent. She closed her eyes, savoring it. Who knew how long it would be before she held her again?

Lily's little hand touched Margot's arm. She opened her eyes and pulled the girl into her embrace, holding both twins close. Kissing them on their blonde heads, she battled back the waterworks. "You two be good for Beth and Dean, okay?" She hoped they didn't cause too many problems. They knew she was leaving, but they were too young to understand she wouldn't be back anytime soon.

With one last kiss, she stood up. A tear slipped out, and she turned away before either child could see.

"How about me? Do I get hugs?" Max caught Margot's eye and winked as he held his arms open for the twins.

She sent him a tremulous smile. He'd noticed her struggle and stepped in to give her a moment. Though she was sure he really did want hugs from the twins. He adored them, and they adored him back.

Both girls hurried over to Max. He scooped one into each arm and stood. "I'm gonna miss you guys. But you'll have fun here. Miss Annabeth and Mr. Dean will spoil you, I'm sure."

Emily leaned in and rested her forehead against his, giving him a big smile. Margot's heart lurched and a pang of what should have been went through it. Tad used to have the same relationship with the girls. He'd been such a great father. And over a year later, she still didn't understand why he gave it all up.

Giving both kids a quick peck on the cheek, Max set them

down. "All right." He turned to Margot. "Let's get going. Ezra's probably waiting."

Margot rolled her lips in, pressing them together. She nodded, then looked at Annabeth. "Thank you again."

"Of course."

Dean came up beside Annabeth and wrapped an arm around her waist. "They might be a little spoiled when you get back." He grinned.

A short chuckle escaped Margot's chest. "I have no doubt."

Max held out a hand to Margot. "You ready?"

She laced her fingers through his, clinging to the strength and support he offered. "Yes."

He tugged her into the kitchen and toward the back door, his eyes on Dean. "We'll keep you posted."

Dean nodded once. "Do that. And if you need anything, reach out."

"You know it." Max opened the door.

With one last glimpse at her babies, Margot left the house. Hopefully, when she returned, she'd have answers as to how their father died and why he left.

Four

Max kept an eye on Margot as they crossed Annabeth's backyard and into hers. She seemed to have gotten a handle on her tears, though she still looked upset. Hopefully, by the time they landed in North Dakota, she'd be ready to tackle whatever waited for them head-on.

Rounding the corner of the house, Max lifted a hand in greeting to Ezra, who leaned against his car.

Ezra pushed off the fender and smiled. "You guys ready?"

"I think so," Max said. "We just need to grab our bags."

"Let's do it, then. I want to be back for dinner tonight."

Max turned to head into the house, but nudged Margot's arm to get her attention. "You can wait in the car if you want. Ezra and I can get the suitcases." There were only two, plus their carry-ons.

"Oh." She glanced at the car, then back at him. "Are you sure?"

"Yes. Go take a moment."

She inhaled a quick breath through her nose. "I'm not a crybaby, I swear."

He gave her a soft smile and touched her arm. "I know

you're not. We all have things that test us. You'll be okay once you get a handle on stuff."

"All of us, huh? Even you?"

Oh, if she only knew. One day, he'd tell her his hang-ups. "Yes. Now go. Sit."

She thrust her tongue into the corner of her mouth, glancing toward the house. Finally, she nodded. "Okay. Thanks."

"Yep." He started for the front door while she headed for the car.

Ezra caught up to him as he crossed the threshold. "She okay?"

"Yeah." Max reached for his suitcase. "She's just upset about leaving the girls."

Understanding lit Ezra's eyes. "Ah. Enough said. I know we can tell her they're in great hands—all of us will watch out for them while she's gone, not just Annabeth and Dean—but it won't matter. Those are her babies."

"Yeah."

"You doing okay?"

Max frowned. "Why wouldn't I be?"

Ezra lifted a shoulder, then slung Margot's carry-on over it. "You're pretty attached to the twins too."

Max's gaze darted to the window overlooking the backyard and Annabeth's house beyond. It bothered him a little that he wouldn't see them for several days, but not like Margot. "I'm good." He picked up his carry-on.

The amusement dancing in Ezra's blue eyes told him he wasn't fooling anyone, but he didn't care. The man could think whatever he wanted. Em and Lily were in good hands, and he had bigger things to worry about.

He hadn't voiced his concerns about Tad's death to anyone, but the guys knew. They felt it too. He'd seen it on Dean's face when they said goodbye. He'd heard it in Ezra's voice when he asked the man to fly them to San José. The circumstances were more than suspicious. And Max had never liked how Tad cut all contact with Margot and the twins. With the way Margot and Annabeth described him, it was wildly out of character. It was his hope that North Dakota would offer some answers, or at least avenues they could go down to find out why he left.

"That everything?" Ezra glanced around.

Max took a quick look. "I think so, yes. Let's go."

They headed for the car, stowing the luggage in the cargo area of the SUV, before climbing inside.

The drive up the coast was an easy one, and they were soon pulling into the airport. Ezra flashed his ID at a guard, who recognized him and waved them through with a smile.

"It's nice knowing people who know people," Margot commented. "I hate airport security."

"I wish I could fly you all the way to North Dakota. But Brooke's got several board members coming in, and she asked me to take them on some helicopter tours, so I'm stuck here." Ezra glanced at her in the rearview mirror.

"It's fine. We'll manage. Going through security alone will be a breeze. I'm upset about leaving the girls behind, but I will not miss lugging a stroller and two cooped-up toddlers through an airport."

Max hid a grin. It'd be more of a breeze than she knew. Their first-class seats meant they could go through the expedited line.

Ezra pulled up near a hangar and parked. Brooke's plane with her company's logo sat outside. For this leg of the trip, Max had insisted on paying for the fuel and Ezra's time. Brooke had protested, but he wouldn't take no for an answer. She did enough for them, and he never wanted her to feel like they took her for granted. She'd sicced Ford on him, but Max had simply handed him the check and told him to do whatever he wanted with it if she wouldn't accept it. Brooke's company had founded a non-profit to help the local impoverished people. He figured Ford would add it to their coffers as an anonymous donation. Margot didn't know he'd paid her, and he didn't intend to enlighten her. He also didn't plan to tell her that the money she gave him for her flight and for the hotel, he'd put into a high-yield savings account. Someday, all the money would go to the twins. He didn't need it.

Getting out, they grabbed their luggage and headed for the plane. Ezra unlocked the cargo compartment, and he and Max stowed the bags. Once that was done, he lowered the stairs. "You two can go get situated. I have to do a few pre-flight checks, then we can get going."

"Sounds good." Max motioned for Margot to precede him onto the plane.

"Where do you want to sit?" She glanced back as she walked into the main cabin.

"Wherever."

She picked two leather seats facing each other, with a small table in between. Stowing their bags, they settled in.

"You know, I don't think I've thanked you for coming with me and for setting all this up." Margot gestured to their surroundings. "Once again, you've put your business on hold to help someone else. Thank you."

He waved a hand, then folded them over his stomach as he relaxed into his seat. While he was independently wealthy thanks to some wise investments with his military retirement and hazard pay, he couldn't sit at home all day and do nothing. The boredom would drive him insane. So, he took tourists on speedboat tours of the coastline and offered parasailing adventures. "It's not a problem. It mostly runs itself. I've hired a great crew. They flew into action when I called and have rearranged the schedule to accommodate my absence. I can keep up with the paperwork while we're gone. It's all online."

"Well, I still appreciate it. I know I balked at you coming, but I'm glad now you didn't listen. I don't want to be alone when I do this."

"I know." He sent her a cocky smile, trying to lighten the mood. "And I knew then too." Honestly, he was a bit uncomfortable with her thanks. He wasn't here for that. He was just here for her.

The team liked to tease him that he had a thing for Margot. He always denied it, said she was just a friend. And that was true. She was his friend. But the truth was, he did have feelings for her. Margot was sweet and kind. Her soft, shy smile had drawn his attention the moment he met her. There was an elegance and a grace about her that just made her—special. As he'd gotten to know her and she'd opened up more, the attraction had only grown. She was brilliant, funny, sassy, and a wonderful mom.

He kept his feelings to himself, though, because he didn't want to make her uncomfortable. When they met, she was reeling from her husband's betrayal. She didn't need some guy fawning all over her. She needed a friend. Someone she could lean on and trust to be there. He'd done everything he could to be that person.

Margot chuckled. "Sometimes, it's scary how well you know me. I mean, I know we spend a decent amount of time together, but we've only known each other a year. There are times where you know what I need before I've even figured out what's wrong."

He lifted a shoulder. "I pay attention. And you can't sit there and tell me you don't know the little quirks about me. Shall I remind you of the Saltillo tile incident?" He arched an eyebrow. She'd let the twins fingerpaint on his Saltillo tile floors. She'd covered the tile with a tarp and paper, but hadn't told him that until after he'd panicked.

She rolled her lips inward, amusement dancing in her eyes

as she tried to suppress a laugh and failed. "Oh yeah. Sometimes, it's just too easy."

"I was sick, too, so more easily fooled."

"Mmm-hmm, sure. Keep telling yourself that."

One side of his mouth lifted. "I will."

They kept their conversation light while they waited on Ezra to finish. Max asked about the progress on the clinic and learned they were closer to being open than he'd thought. It would be a great asset to the community, for the rural populations, especially, once it opened. Soon, they'd be hiring office staff, then clinical staff.

When Ezra ascended the steps and closed the door, Max was happy to see some of the sadness had left Margot's eyes.

"All right, let's get in the air, shall we?" Ezra stepped toward the cockpit. "If you need something, just come up front. There are drinks in the fridge here." He pointed to a panel on the wall. "And snacks in the cabinets. It's a quick flight, so we should be there shortly."

"Thanks, Ezra," Max said. "I think we'll be fine."

With a nod, Ezra disappeared.

True to his word, the flight was quick. About an hour after they took off, they touched down in San José. Max helped Margot down the steep stairs, then they retrieved their bags from the cargo hold. They piled into a car near the hangar, and Ezra drove them to the international terminal. Pulling into the drop-off lane, he parked, then helped Max retrieve the bags from the trunk.

"That's everything." Ezra held out a hand to Max. "Safe travels. If you need anything, let us know."

Clasping his hand, Max gave him a quick smile. "We will, thanks."

"Anytime." Smiling, Ezra turned to Margot. He leaned in and gave her a quick hug. "I hope things turn out well. You've got good company." He pulled back to wink at Max.

To Max's surprise, Margot sent him a sunny smile. "I know."

Ezra lifted an eyebrow and sent him a curious look before a bright smile crossed his face. He shut the trunk, casting a quick look back.

"We'll see you in a few days." Max caught the slightly rascally look in his eyes. He backed away, towing his suitcase, and ignored it.

"Yep. Let me know when your return flight is. I'll do my best to pick you up from here."

"Will do."

Margot lifted a hand. "Thanks, Ezra."

He nodded once. "See ya." Rounding the rear of the car, he opened the driver's door and climbed in while Max led Margot away.

FIVE

Margot shifted, doing her best to stay awake. They were on the last leg of their flight, and she was ready to be done. But she didn't want to sleep yet. If she took a nap now, it would just take her longer to wind down once they got to the hotel, and it was already late. She just wanted to go to bed and not wake up until morning. Not lie there, tossing and turning because she wasn't sleepy enough thanks to her nap. The oversize first-class seat was making it hard for her to stay awake, though. She had ample room to stretch out and not bump into anyone. For once, she wanted the cramped space of economy seating.

Next to her, Max yawned. At least she wasn't the only one who was tired. He'd stifled several yawns since they took off from Denver.

The plane's engine noise changed, and she felt it tilt down slightly. *Thank God.* They were beginning their descent.

A yawn stole over her face. She smothered it behind her hand, then blinked away the moisture that gathered in her eyes. "Oh, this is ridiculous." She shifted again, turning toward Max. "Distract me, so I stay awake."

The smile that ghosted over his handsome face ticked her heart rate up, banishing a bit of her sleepiness. Max was dangerous to her equilibrium when she was wide awake and could shore up all her walls. But tired? She didn't have the energy to patch the cracks that formed whenever those crinkle lines appeared next to his eyes when he smiled.

"Read any good books lately?"

Margot laughed. "That was so not what I expected you to say."

He chuckled. "What did you think I'd say?"

"I don't know. Not that."

"It's still a valid question."

"It is. The answer is I can't remember the last time I read a book for fun."

His eyebrows shot up. "Seriously?"

"Yes. After work, I'm busy with the girls. Once they're in bed, I do whatever chores I didn't get done while they were awake, then either do a little reading for work—or do some actual work—then take a shower and go to sleep."

"What about the weekends? I mean, I know you and Annabeth have been doing some work then, but you don't work all day, every day."

"No, you're right. But I spend as much time with Emily and Lily on the weekends as I can. We go to the beach or to one of the animal sanctuaries. Sometimes we go shopping and get some fresh, local ingredients and make simple things they can help with. I don't really have free time right now. I also don't remember the last time I watched something on TV that wasn't a cartoon."

"You watched the World Series with me and the others last month." He'd extended an open invitation to everyone for every game of the series. She'd come over a couple of times.

"Sort of. I spent a lot of time in your pool." The twins had wanted to swim, and Margot really didn't have much interest in baseball.

"True. I guess I didn't realize how busy life with toddlers is. I mean, I know it's crazy, but not, no free time crazy."

"It is what it is, Max." Even when Tad was still in the picture, she'd had little time to herself. Any extra time she had away from the girls was taken up by her work schedule. She actually preferred her busy life now. As crazy as it was, it was less stressful because she was out of the hospital's fast-paced environment.

His hand covered hers. Margot's damn heart sped up again and more cracks appeared in her walls.

"You need to take care of yourself, Margot. How about we set up a day each week where I take the kids and you do whatever you want? No cleaning." He shook a finger at her. "Sleeping, reading, watching TV, anything that involves you doing something you want. Not something you need to do."

That sounded wonderful, but she and her daughters weren't his problem. They were no one's problem. She waved a hand, dismissing his suggestion. "I'll be fine. Eventually, they won't need me so much, and I'll be able to do more."

He snagged her hand as it fluttered back to her lap. "Before or after you become a shell of yourself?"

She yanked her hand away and scowled. "My life and my problems are just that. Mine. Stop worrying about me."

"I don't want to."

"Try."

"No."

She let out a little huff. Why did he have to be so stubborn? "This is not the sort of distraction I was talking about when I asked you to keep me awake. Why don't you want to?"

"Because I care about you. You're my friend, and I don't want to see you work yourself to the bone when you have help available. I understand more now, since you told me about your parents, why you want to go it alone, but you are not them. Neither am I, nor are any of the rest of us."

Her scowl softened but didn't disappear. "I know that."

"Logically, yes. But in there?" He tapped her chest, just above her heart. "I don't think you do."

She did not want to psychoanalyze herself right now. Not ever, if she was honest. But especially not when she was so tired. "How about we talk about something else?"

He sighed and sank back into his seat. "You didn't like my topic of conversation, so you pick."

"Okay, how about you tell me about the things that test you?"

He groaned. "What is this? Confession time?"

"Hey, you wanted to pick apart my deepest fears. It's only fair I get to do the same."

The side glance he sent her spoke volumes about his lack of desire to talk about himself. She wasn't sorry. Turnabout was fair play. If he didn't want to talk about himself, that was fine. But he couldn't expect her to if he didn't.

"Tight spaces."

Margot's brows dipped. "What?"

"Something that tests me. Tight spaces."

Dammit. He wanted to talk. "You don't have to tell me."

"But I do if I ever want you to talk to me and to let me into that impermeable bubble you surround yourself with."

"What are you talking about? I let you in." Of all the adults in her life, besides Annabeth, she was closest to him.

"You let me into the outer bubble. But there's an inner one that only the girls and Annabeth are in. And even then, I'm not sure that Annabeth doesn't have one foot on the outside."

She really hated how perceptive he was. Or maybe she just couldn't hide her feelings as well as she thought she could. Annabeth always called her on her BS too. He wasn't wrong, though. She did keep most people at a distance. It was safer that way. "We're not talking about me. How about we don't talk about you, either? I'm awake enough now."

Max raked a hand through his dark blond hair. "Margot..." Exasperation colored his tone.

Feeling like a bit of a bitch, she flapped a hand and leaned her head back, closing her eyes. "I'm sorry for snapping at you." To her horror, she felt tears pressing against her eyelids. She turned toward the window. "I'm exhausted and stressed out. Diving into my feelings is not something I can handle right now."

Max's warm hand enveloped hers. A tear slid free from her eye. She let it go, not wanting to draw attention to it, but he saw it anyway.

"Hey, it's okay. Come here." He tugged her closer, tipping her into his chest.

For a fraction of a second, she resisted. But then the spicy scent of his soap and something that was all Max hit her. Her resistance crumbled, and she melted into him as best she could with the armrest digging into her side. What she did to deserve this man, she didn't know. He'd been such a wonderful friend this past year. A rock in the storm. She appreciated his presence, but she hadn't been as kind about accepting it as she could have been. Instead, she did some beating on the rock. But he hadn't chipped or wavered. At least, not outwardly. She was starting to see now that maybe there were some internal cracks appearing, but she didn't know how to let her walls down and let him in.

One thing was certain, though. She needed to figure it out soon before she hit too hard, and he broke and walked away.

Maybe it was inevitable. Everyone had walked away from her. Except Annabeth. She was the sister Margot never had.

Could Max be the brother?

The thought no sooner entered her mind than she

dismissed it. She was too attracted to Max to think of him as a brother.

At the core of things, that was what held her back from letting him into her so-called inner bubble. The last man she'd been attracted to—the one who was supposed to love and support her for the rest of her life—had thrown her life into the spin cycle without warning. She wasn't sure she could handle that again.

But being in Max's arms sure felt nice. The comfort level he provided was off the charts. Not to mention the low hum of attraction that thrummed through her veins. She liked that too, even if she didn't feel ready to act on it.

"I never cared much for dark rooms and elevators when I was a kid." Max's soft voice broke through her thoughts. His warm breath ruffled the hair at her temple. "They freaked me out a little. My mom, she always made sure I had a nightlight. As an adult now, I don't close the curtains all the way, and I take the stairs a lot."

Margot sniffed, curling her fingers into his shirt. She knew what he was doing. He was distracting her by continuing like nothing was wrong. It was an out she'd happily take. She simply didn't have the bandwidth for her emotions at the moment. "How is that something that tests you?"

He raised a hand, stroking her hair. "You didn't let me finish."

"Oh, sorry." The slightest smile curled her lip.

His chuckle rumbled under her ear. "Those things are fairly minor. A lot of people don't like the dark or elevators, but they handle them fine. I do, too, usually. But there's a reason I have a house with a wall of windows. Why I prefer speedboats to Ford's fishing vessels."

The hand wrapped around her shoulders gripped her sleeve for a moment before it relaxed. "About a year before I retired from the Air Force, I was involved in a training accident."

"What?" Margot sat up to look at him. "I didn't know that."

"It's not something I talk about much. The guys know, but it's just not something that comes up in casual conversation, you know?"

She could understand that. "So, what happened?"

"You know I was a pararescueman."

She nodded.

"We were up with a group of PJ candidates, and one of them didn't want to jump. Even though he'd jumped before, this time was different because we were near water. Navigating away from obstacles is something they need to know how to do, and this guy—well, the thing that tested him was water."

"Was it deep water?"

Max shrugged. "Deep enough. It was a small lake, and we were close enough to shore, gliding to safety wasn't terribly difficult. And for the record, it isn't like we just throw everyone out of the plane and there's no one on the ground in case something goes wrong when we do these jumps. On this exercise, we had a boat in the water and a team on the shoreline. But this guy didn't see any of that. He just looked out and saw water and panicked. Anyway, on our training flights, everyone jumps. If you're in that plane, unless you're unconscious and/or dying, you jump. If you don't, you lose your jump status."

The flight attendant walked by with a trash bag, interrupting them for a moment. Margot gathered the trash from her earlier snack and passed it over. Once the man moved on, Max continued.

"Part of my job was to make sure everyone jumped. I got him moving toward the exit, got him to stop clinging to the door, but he still just stood there. There were two more behind him, plus me, so I slid in behind him to scream at him to move his ass one way or another, and he turned before I could utter a word. I don't know if he thought I was going to shove him out or what, but his eyes went huge behind his goggles and he shot a hand out and grabbed onto my harness. It caught me by surprise, and I stumbled forward. We were close enough to the door that my momentum carried us out of the plane." He stopped for a second, his jaw muscles working.

Margot put her hand on his forearm and gave it a gentle squeeze. "You don't have to continue."

"It's okay. I want you to know about it." He covered her hand, then laced their fingers. "When we cleared the plane, he still had a death grip on me. I don't know if you've ever noticed, but sky divers fall a certain way to maintain control. With him latched on to me like a monkey, neither of us could do that, so we just tumbled through the air. Several times a second, I'd catch a glimpse of the lake, and I knew from experience that I had a certain amount of time to get him off and deploy my canopy before our auto-deploy devices would go off."

"Auto-deploy device? What's that?" Margot frowned. She'd never heard of such a thing. A backup chute, sure, but not an auto-deploy chute.

"A lot of skydivers have three parachutes now. A main, a reserve, and an auto-deploy. The latter goes off without any input from the diver if it detects an unsafe rate of descent at a certain distance above the ground."

"Oh. I suppose that's a good thing."

"Usually, but if we'd stayed locked together, it could have caused issues for us both. That canopy is on our chest."

Her nose wrinkled. "Oh... yeah."

"Exactly. This guy had locked his hands around my harness like some sort of pneumatic device and the hydraulics were broken. My options were to knock him out, or somehow get him off before the devices blew."

"You couldn't just pull your main chute? That's on your back, right?"

"Yes, but our canopies operated with a pilot chute, not a ripcord. It's basically a small parachute you pull from a pouch and release into the airstream. It inflates and the drag then releases the main canopy. I couldn't get to mine or his."

"Geez." She stared at him with wide eyes. "So, how did you get free?"

"I grabbed his goggles and yanked them off his face. It startled him enough that he let go. We were at the point of no return by then. I had seconds before my auto-deploy device would go off, so I arched my back to stop my tumble. The moment I had a modicum of stability, I deployed my main canopy."

"You landed in the water, didn't you?"

"Yeah. And hard enough to stun me momentarily. I didn't react with enough speed to avoid getting tangled in the canopy and its lines."

"Oh, God, Max. That's terrifying."

"It wasn't pleasant. But that's why I like tight spaces less now than ever. That parachute wrapped around me, and I couldn't battle my way out of it. If the patrol boat hadn't been watching the action and wasn't right there when I landed, I'd have been at the bottom of the lake."

"Did the other guy make it?"

Max rolled his lips in and looked away briefly. "No. The guys on the ground said after we broke apart, he continued to cartwheel. When his safety canopy auto-deployed, the bundle hit him in the face. Ironically, he landed on the shore, but he hit the ground, unconscious, at about forty miles an hour."

Margot shook her head. "That's terrible. Why is it the dark and tight spaces bother you, though, and not the water?"

"Probably just the claustrophobic nature of things. I've always been a good swimmer, and I was a certified scuba diver, so I knew not to panic, and I could hold my breath for a couple of minutes. It was enough for the team to raise me above the surface so I could breathe while they cut me loose. I was trapped in the canopy fabric a lot longer than I was underwater."

"I cannot imagine what that was like. I'm sorry you went through that. Were you okay, physically, afterward?"

"I broke a few ribs and my left leg just below my knee. And I had a concussion. Nothing that didn't heal."

"Still, the psychological impact—you're still dealing with that."

"To a degree, sure. I don't turn into a crazy man in an elevator or in a dark room, though. It just makes me uncomfortable. More so than I ever was as a child."

She tipped her head. "That's why you don't like my house, isn't it? It's too cramped."

He grimaced. "It's not my favorite place, no. You've done a great job making it yours, and it looks nice, but yeah. I prefer my house."

Margot chuckled. "I prefer your house, too, but not because it's more open. It's just nicer. If I ever decide to quit medicine, I'm going to beg you to let me open a catering business from your kitchen."

The sadness left his eyes as he smiled at her. "You can come cook there anytime you want. I only ask you leave a plate for me in the fridge. Especially if you make that seafood linguine you made that one night when Edie's family was down." He rolled his eyes back and moaned. "You could serve it on a plate made of bark and I would lick it clean."

She patted his shoulder, laughing, as she turned and sat back in her seat. "My Neanderthal man."

"Hey, sometimes caveman tactics are the only way to go," he said, chuckling along with her.

Their light conversation continued as the plane descended into the Minot airport. Margot had found a second wind that was enough to get her through disembarking and finding their luggage at the baggage claim.

"Let's get our car and get the heck out of here." Max raised the handle on his suitcase and glanced overhead at the signs pointing the way to the car rental counters.

"Yes, please. Although, I'm not sure I want to go outside. Did you hear the captain's announcement on the local weather when we landed? We need to dig out our coats before we leave the terminal." She'd nearly swallowed her tongue when she heard the current temperature.

Three degrees.

Three.

It was barely past Thanksgiving. It should not be allowed to be that cold yet. But there was a silver lining. It wasn't snowing. That was already on the ground in giant piles. She'd seen it when they'd taxied in.

"You can do that while I get the car."

"Deal." Dragging her case behind her, she followed him to the rental counter. "Give me your suitcase."

He spun it around and leaned the handle toward her. She took it and walked toward the wall, where she was out of the way, and laid the cases down, unzipping hers first. When she packed, she'd put the balled-up parka right in front, knowing she'd need it before she left the airport. She was just happy she had one. In Texas, she didn't need it. But after moving to Ohio last year before she went to Costa Rica, she'd been forced to buy one. Now, she was immensely happy she'd opted for a packable one.

After zipping her case closed again, she opened Max's. Or she tried. He had a lock on it.

Blowing her hair back, she looked up. "Hey, what's the code for your lock?"

He glanced over. "What?"

She held up the locked zipper. "Code?"

"Oh. It's the girls' birthday. Month and day."

Margot blinked at him, disbelief short-circuiting her brain. Why would he do that?

He seemed to read the question on her face, because he answered before she could ask. "When I flew to the States to help Sam, you guys were at the house while I packed. Emily wanted to help, and she was fascinated by the lock, so I reset it to show her how it worked and just used her birthday."

Tipping her head, she nodded. "That makes sense." She spun the dial and opened the lock. Flipping the case open, she couldn't stop the little laugh that escaped. Like his house, his suitcase was neat as a pin. Packing cubes filled the space, and she could see through the mesh that every item was folded and rolled. She picked up the pack that contained his coat, removing it before putting the bag back and closing the case.

Coats in hand, she wandered over to him. "Here."

"Thanks." He took the coat and shrugged it over his shoulders while the clerk finished the paperwork.

Margot put hers on and huddled into it, anticipating the cold that would blast her in the face when she stepped outside. She wanted to go home.

"Okay, this is the damage and insurance waiver. I just need you to initial it." The young man pushed a contract across the counter at Max.

He picked up a pen and scrawled his initials in the boxes. "Can you add her to the rental?" He pointed the pen at Margot.

"Of course." The man looked at her. "I just need your driver's license, ma'am."

Margot swung her bag off her shoulder and dug inside for

her wallet. She found her Costa Rican license and her passport since she had an international license and handed them over.

It took the man a minute or so to enter her information, then he moved the insurance waiver across the counter to her. "Initial next to him."

Once that was taken care of, he handed her documents back, then set another contract on the counter and asked them to sign it. With the paperwork done, he handed Max a set of keys.

"Your car is in the rental lot. Just follow the signs." The man smiled. "Have a good trip."

Margot offered him a tight smile and pushed away from the desk.

Max gathered up the paperwork. "Thanks." Taking his suitcase from her, he turned, and they headed for the door.

The closer they got to the exit, the chillier the air became. Margot slid her zipper higher. She'd forgotten her gloves. They were still buried in her bag. Her hands would be numb by the time they reached the car.

Reaching the exit, the doors swished open and icy-cold air smacked her in the face. Her shoulders fell. This would not be fun.

Max took her free hand. "Don't think, Margot. Just walk."

Ducking her head, she let him pull her into the arctic air.

Instantly, the tip of her nose turned cold. Her tropical blood was too thin to keep it warm. She was glad she'd left her hair down to cover her ears, or she was sure they'd suffer the same fate.

The walk to the car wasn't terrible, but it still stretched into an eternity. Her teeth chattered like castanets by the time Max found the SUV he rented.

It beeped as he unlocked the doors.

"Get in and start it. I'll stow our bags." He handed her the keys.

Margot scurried around to the driver's side and got in. Stepping on the brake, she pushed the start button. The engine started without a hiccup. She fiddled with the dials on the dash and soon had the heat on high. The back hatch closed as she got out. Just because she signed the contract didn't mean she wanted to drive.

Rounding the rear of the car, she practically dove into the passenger seat. She shut her door with a slam and lifted her hands to her mouth to blow on them. "I'm gonna need a heavier coat. This one's for Ohio cold, not North Dakota cold."

"You need gloves too."

"They're in my bag. I forgot to get them out."

"I'm betting they're not warm enough, either. But hang in there. You'll be standing in a hot shower in just a few minutes. Minot's not that large."

She buckled her seatbelt as he pulled out of the parking space, then pulled her hands inside her coat sleeves. "Did you look it up before we came?"

"No. I've been here before."

"You have? When?"

"Maybe seven or eight years ago. There's an Air Force base here. It was for an exercise we ran with their bomber wing. It was cold, then, too."

"I know we just talked about it on the plane, but I still always forget you were military. And elite military at that. You scream rich island boy now. No offense."

"None taken. I'm retired and enjoying the slower life." He turned out of the lot and onto the main road.

"I'd be so bored if I retired at your age. I don't know what it's like to not be busy."

"I'm not exactly idle." He glanced side to side at the end of the road, then turned onto the highway.

"That's true." He had his business, and there were all the protection jobs he took on with his friends.

"It is different, though; you're right. I have time to be lazy, but the biggest change is that the work isn't as strenuous or stressful. Don't get me wrong. I'm an adrenaline junkie, but I just reached a point where I couldn't do it anymore. That accident had a lot to do with it. I could still jump, but some of the thrill was gone. I'd been in over twenty years by then, so retiring made sense."

"Is that why you went to Costa Rica too? Everyone else ended up down there to deal with emotional trauma, it seems."

He lifted a shoulder. "Sort of. I went back to North Carolina, where I'm from, first. Then my mom died. There wasn't anything to hold me to anyplace anymore. Ford's an old friend from a joint op, and we'd kept in touch. He sent flowers when my mom passed away and an email extending an invitation to come visit him whenever I wanted. I took him up on it and I just found... peace. The next thing I knew, I was applying for residency status down there and selling everything."

"It's a giant leap of faith, isn't it? Moving to another country."

"Hell yes. But it was the right decision." He glanced at her. "Has it been for you?"

Margot shrugged one shoulder and looked out her window at the darkened city. "So far, yes." Her daughters were happy and thriving, she had a career that looked nothing like she planned, but she loved it anyway, and she had Annabeth and all their other friends. But there was still a piece of her that was bruised. She didn't think she'd fully mourned the life she'd given up. One day, she would. But she needed time and answers. Hopefully, she'd get the latter tomorrow.

Max turned into a well-lit parking lot of an extended-stay

hotel. He found a space as close to the door as possible, and they hurried through the frigid winter air to the front door.

She sighed as they stepped inside. The lobby was toasty warm. She unzipped her coat.

A middle-aged woman came out from the office behind the front desk and offered them a cheery smile. "Hello. Checking in?"

"Yes." Max stepped forward. "We have reservations. Max Carson?"

The woman typed his name into the computer. "Yep. Two king rooms?"

"Yes." Max reached into his pocket for his wallet and handed her his ID. "Can they be adjoining or very close to each other?"

"Let me check." The woman turned back to her computer. A few moments later, she nodded. "That won't be a problem."

Margot breathed a sigh of relief. She didn't know why, but the thought of being on another floor or the opposite end of the hall from Max bugged her. It was probably just the circumstances of the trip. The whole situation had her weirded out.

The check-in process was a quick one, and soon they had their keys and were on the elevator, heading up to their rooms.

Every step Margot took as they walked down the hall made the fatigue she'd banished grow heavier. It was like her body and brain knew that the sweet bliss of sleep was only feet away now.

"This is us." Max paused outside a pair of doors.

Sure enough, the number on the wall matched the number written on the little folder the desk clerk had handed her. She withdrew a keycard and held it up to the reader. The door snicked and the light turned green. She twisted the handle and pushed it open. "I'll see you in the morning."

They'd already planned to meet for breakfast about eight a.m. They had to meet the detective at nine.

"Margot."

Max's hand on her jacket stopped her from going inside. She looked up at him through bleary eyes.

"Will you be all right tonight?"

The simple question broke through her wall. She felt the press of tears against the backs of her eyes again. She wanted to lean into him and let him hold her all night, but she didn't dare. Getting any closer to Max than she already was would just add to how overwhelmed she already felt. Right now, she needed to concentrate on Tad and straightening out the mess he'd left behind.

So, she nodded and pushed the door open wider. "I'm okay. Have a good night." Without waiting for an answer, she escaped into her room, hearing him call a soft goodnight as the door closed.

Margot closed her eyes, squeezing out a couple of tears.

How did her life get so complicated?

Six

ot coffee seared Max's tongue. Wincing, he blew on the fragrant brew as he leaned against the wall in the hotel's breakfast area, waiting on Margot. He'd been up for nearly two hours. So far, he'd been for a run in the hotel's fitness center and had a shower. He probably should have slept longer, but after being stationary so long yesterday because of all the traveling, he'd needed the physical movement. He wanted to swim, but that would have to wait until he returned home. The hotel's small pool wasn't open at the hours he wanted to exercise, and when it was, it was filled with children. There was nothing wrong with that, but he had no desire to dodge kids doing cannonballs while he swam laps.

His stomach growled. Margot needed to hurry up. If she took much longer, he was going to eat without her.

Crossing his ankles, Max took another sip of his coffee and wrinkled his nose. It needed cream.

Movement in his peripheral vision caught his attention, and he glanced up to see Margot rounding the corner into the dining area. He pushed away from the wall, smiling as he studied her face. She looked perkier, and her expression was no longer pinched or sad. Apparently, the rest had done her some good.

"Good morning." She returned his smile with a sunny one of her own.

"Morning." He raised his coffee cup in greeting. "You look like you got some rest."

"I did. I washed off the travel grunge, then went right to sleep. But I could still use some of that." She pointed at his cup.

Max nodded toward the large coffee urn. "Make sure you leave room for cream. It's pretty bitter."

"Good to know. Ooo, waffles." She bypassed the coffee for the waffle maker.

His chuckle was low as he followed her into the buffet area. She was much more herself this morning. Whether that was due to the rest or she'd just shored up her walls, he didn't know. Probably a bit of both. Hopefully, whatever it was, it would get her through their meeting with the detective.

Breakfast was a quick affair, neither of them wanting to linger. Max, too, had a waffle, which was surprisingly good, though he wished they had real syrup instead of the pre-packaged, artificially flavored stuff. Along with eggs and some bacon, he had a full belly and was ready for the day.

Except he needed better coffee. Grimacing, he tossed his cup in the trash, along with his napkin, then turned to Margot. "We need to get real coffee before we meet with the police."

"Agreed. Even with cream, this isn't very good. It tastes burned." Her cup landed next to his in the bin. "Let's go."

Leaving the dining area, they walked through the lobby and exited the front door. Ice cold air and a fine snow sandblasted Max's face. He hunched his shoulders, trying to shield his ears. Man, it was cold here.

Beside him, Margot shivered. "I definitely need a better coat."

"If we have to stay very long, or spend a lot of time outside, we'll get you one. For now, I think you'll be okay. Although, it wouldn't be a bad idea to get better gloves. I didn't bring the right ones, either." He held up a glove-covered hand and flexed his fingers. They were meant for a normal, run-of-the-mill chill. Not the deep freeze.

"Let's see what the detective has to say, then we'll figure it out. Unlock the doors before I turn into a popsicle." She sped up, heading for their car.

Max pressed the button on the fob in his pocket. The car locks clicked open as she reached the vehicle. In one smooth movement, she opened the door and slid inside. Max wasn't far behind her.

Cranking the engine, he let it heat up for a minute, steeling himself to go out and scrape the frost off the windows. For a moment, he debated letting the defrost do the work, but that would take several minutes. And he really did want better coffee.

Gritting his teeth, he hopped out. After finding the ice scraper in the rear cargo area, he set to work, stopping every so often to flex his fingers. The wind just cut right through his thin gloves.

Once he had the windows clear enough he could see, he practically dove into the car.

Handing Margot the ice scraper, he rubbed his hands together for warmth, then buckled up. "Ready?"

She set the bit of plastic at her feet. "Yes."

"Let's go, then." Putting the car in gear, he pulled out of his parking spot and they were on their way.

One quick stop at a coffee kiosk later for two small coffees, they turned into the sheriff's department.

"Maybe we should have gotten the coffee after our meeting." Margot set her cup in the cup holder. "I can't drink all this now. It's too hot. It'll be cold when we come back out. Or should we take it in?"

"Let's leave it here. Even cold, it'll be better than the swill at the hotel." He took one last sip of his coffee, then set it next to hers.

They headed inside, giving their names to the deputy manning the desk and telling him who they were there to see. He gave them visitor's badges and led them down a hallway to a small conference room.

"Detective Sorenson will be in soon," the deputy said. Backing out of the room, he closed the door.

Max pulled out a chair for Margot, then sat next to her. She folded her hands in her lap and stared out the window. A moment later, she crossed her legs and arms, only to uncross them and fold her hands in her lap again. Her knee bounced.

Hoping to still the thoughts he could practically hear racing through her mind, Max covered her hands. Immediately, she flipped one over and laced their fingers. The knee bouncing stopped.

They sat in silence for several minutes, the tick... tick... tick... of the clock on the wall the only sound. Five minutes after they sat down, the door opened again, and two men stepped in.

The smile of greeting on the first man's face took on a slight curiousness as his gaze landed on Max. "Hello. I'm Detective Sorenson. This is Agent Gallagher from the FBI."

Max's gaze sharpened.

FBI?

He'd been right to come with Margot. It seemed her ex-husband's case was more serious than they thought.

"Max Carson." He stood and held out a hand. "I'm a friend of Margot's."

"Nice to meet you." Sorenson shook his hand, then turned to Margot. "Mrs. Gaultier."

"It's Dr. Gaultier. And it's nice to meet you too." She rose halfway from her chair and shook his hand, then the agent's, before sitting down.

Max nodded to the agent, then reclaimed his seat. He pinned a look on Detective Sorenson. "Unless Margot forgot to mention it, she didn't say anything about meeting with a federal agent, in addition to you."

"Professional courtesy. I decided to include him in this interview since the vehicle that led us to Dr. Gaultier was found on federal land. She didn't mention she was bringing you along, either." Sorenson took a seat and scooted closer to the table. He set down the file folder he carried and flipped it open as he looked at Margot. "First, I would like to say thank you for coming all this way. It's not lost on us that you took an international flight for a man you're no longer married to."

"Thank you," Margot said.

She'd folded her hands in her lap again and was alternating which one was on top. Max once more wrapped a hand over hers. Her fingers stilled beneath his, and she sent him a small smile.

"These are the items we found in the car that we'd like you to identify." Sorenson spread several pictures over the table.

Margot leaned forward to get a closer look. So did Max.

In the first picture, a basic watch sat open inside an evidence bag on a table. What made it notable was the Texas A&M cloth watchband. The second picture was of a hat emblazoned with the name of a medical system. The third picture made Max's heart stutter. It was a picture of Emily and Lily when they were about a year old.

"These are your daughters, yes?" Sorenson tapped the picture of the twins.

Margot rolled her lips inward, pressing them together so

tightly the skin around them turned white. She clutched Max's fingers and nodded. "Yes," she whispered.

"And what about the items in the other pictures? Do you recognize anything there?"

Again, she nodded. "He got that watch when we were in residency. Same with the hat. That's the hospital we worked at."

"Can you tell us what happened?" Max asked.

Sorenson and Agent Gallagher shared a quick glance, then the latter spoke.

"Dr. Gaultier, when was the last time you spoke to your husband?"

Max ground his back teeth together. He should have brought his attorney along. They'd dodged the question.

Margot's brow furrowed. "Before work the day he left us. And he's my ex-husband. We're divorced."

"You haven't spoken to him since he left you? How did you divorce, then?" Gallagher asked.

"He left divorce papers on the counter with a note, asking me to tell the girls he loved them. I tried contacting him through the attorney's office listed on the documents, but he never responded. He'd already signed them, giving up everything he didn't take with him, including custody of the twins. The only thing I really wanted him to take possession of was his car, but once it became apparent even his attorneys couldn't contact him, I dropped that and just signed on the dotted line."

Sorenson frowned. "So, the car we found isn't his?"

"It might be, but it's not the one he had when we were married. I sold it and paid off the loan. How did you know to contact me?"

"We found fingerprints in the car that came back to his name. A quick background check revealed his marriage to you and your daughters. With your confirmation of those items"

—he pointed to the photos—"we're fairly certain the man we found is your ex. The DNA sample you submitted from one of your daughters should give us a positive ID." Sorenson twirled his pen between his hands.

Max's frown deepened. "You know, I understand why you wanted her to look at the photographs and confirm that those things belong to Tad, but with the DNA sample from Lily, why did you need us to come here? We could have done all of this over Zoom."

Again, Sorenson and Gallagher exchanged a look.

A hollow pit formed in Max's stomach, and suddenly, he knew his previous suspicions were correct. "You think Tad was murdered, don't you?"

SEVEN

Margot couldn't stop the gasp that escaped at Max's question. With wide eyes, she looked at him. "What?" Her gaze shot to Sorenson. "Is he right?"

The detective looked at Gallagher again, and she snapped.

"Stop silently talking. Answer my question. Was Tad murdered?"

"Dr. Gaultier—"

She held up a hand. "I am here voluntarily, and as you said, I came a long way. If you want me to answer any more of your questions, you need to answer mine." She was done with their runaround. Honestly, she should have asked for more information when Sorenson asked her to come up, but she'd been too shocked by the news of Tad's death. The idea he'd been murdered had rumbled around in the back of her mind, considering the condition they found him in, but hearing it out loud was jarring. And it was enough to snap her out of the nervous state she'd been in.

"Yes," Gallagher answered. "We think he was murdered."

"Why?" Max countered.

The agent's gaze bounced between him and Margot for

several moments. "An ice fisherman found his body. Snagged his line on it."

Sorenson took over. "When we got there, we widened the hole in the ice to get him out and it was quickly apparent he didn't fall in and drown. He was bundled in plastic and rope. We think he was tied to something to keep him down."

Margot felt the color drain from her face. A chill that rivaled the one outside settled into her bones. It was like watching a movie where mobsters murdered their mark and tossed him into the river. That didn't happen in her world.

She sucked in a deep breath through her nose and looked away, covering her mouth. Her hand trembled violently, and her heart raced as jumbled thoughts tumbled through her mind. How could this have happened? Who could have done this? And why?

Max spun her chair so she faced him and put his free hand on her knee. "Hey. Margot, honey. Look at me."

With watery blue eyes, she met his gaze.

"Are you all right? They don't have to continue. We can leave."

For several interminable moments, she stared at him, focusing on the furrows formed on his face by his concerned frown.

Something shifted in her as the deep concern in his expression registered. She couldn't imagine facing this without Max. He was like an anchor for her emotions. His supportive presence was something she could yank on and strain against, but was always steady. Always there to keep her from getting completely lost. Somewhere along the line, he'd become essential to her well-being. That should scare her and make her want to back away—considering how she'd been burned by Tad—but it didn't.

Max was built differently. Letting her down, letting anyone down, wasn't something he would ever voluntarily do.

In the last year, he'd proven time and again he'd stand by her side. That he'd give up his time and even put his health on the line to take care of her and the girls.

She shouldn't be surprised at the connection they'd formed. Or that he was so attuned to her.

Drawing on the calmness Max exuded, she drew in another deep, steadying breath and squeezed his hands. "I'm okay," she whispered.

Feeling stronger, she turned to the detective. "I'm sorry. It's just a bit of a shock."

"I understand. I'm sorry for your loss. Do you want me to continue?"

"Yes. Please. I want to know what happened."

He nodded once. "All right. So, when we got your ex-husband's body back to the medical examiner's office, the M.E. noted what looked like several stab wounds to the chest area of his clothing. He was wrapped tightly enough to keep his remains together, but not tightly enough to prevent small aquatic animals from getting in. Between them and the bacteria that are responsible for decay, the M.E. couldn't match any wounds on the body to the holes in the shirt. He did, however, find a small nick on a rib."

Margot sniffed and wiped at her eyes. "I don't understand. Why would someone want to stab Tad? He was a nice guy."

"Even though he left you with no warning?"

"I didn't say there wasn't any warning."

"What exactly happened between you two?" Gallagher asked.

Margot looked away, gathering her thoughts. She'd tried not to think about the end of her marriage too much. At first, it was just too painful. Later, it became something she didn't want to dwell on because she'd rather just move on.

"Early last year, he changed." She dabbed at the corner of her eye with the back of her hand, wiping away the moisture that had formed, then met Gallagher's gaze. "I can't really pinpoint a time or an event, but he just... changed. He became more withdrawn from me and the girls and spent more time away from home. I thought maybe he was cheating, you know? That's what a woman typically thinks when her husband says he has to work late again and again, right? Particularly after you talk to his boss and discover he was barely finishing out his shifts. According to his division chief, Tad would leave as soon as humanly possible. But I wouldn't see him at home until hours later."

"Did you ever ask your husband about it?" Detective Sorenson asked.

She swung her gaze to him. "Only about the lateness. Before I talked to his chief. Tad told me it was research keeping him at work late. But his chief said he didn't know of any projects Tad was working on. That's when he mentioned he'd been practically running out of the hospital at the end of each shift. Tad left before I could work up the courage to ask why he lied."

"Dr. Gaultier, could you tell us about your ex-husband?" Gallagher asked.

Tipping her head, she frowned. "That's a broad question, Agent Gallagher. I can tell you a lot of things. Where would you like me to start?"

"What was he like? Did he have any hobbies or interests?"

"Tad is—was"—*God, how could he be dead?*—"on the quieter side. He was kind. Smart. A good dad. The girls adored him. As far as hobbies go, he liked to golf and play basketball."

Gallagher glanced up from taking notes. "Did he have friends he played with regularly?"

"A few."

"Did any of them ever notice anything was wrong? Maybe

he confided in them that he planned to leave," the agent continued.

"If he did, they didn't say anything to me. But I haven't had much contact with his friends since he left. A lot of them didn't know, either. He ghosted everyone, not just me."

The two men looked at each other, doing that silent talking thing again. This time, Margot didn't mind as much. She could read their look. It said they were as perplexed by Tad's behavior as she was.

"Dr. Gaultier, did your ex have any habits that others would... look down on? Like drinking or drugs? Gambling?" Gallagher asked.

Margot started to shake her head, then paused and looked at Max.

"What?" Sorenson said. "What did he say?"

It was her turn to do some silent communicating. She wasn't sure how much info they should give the authorities about Asher's activities.

Max understood her dilemma and answered for her.

"We have a friend who is very good at sourcing information." He laid a hand on the table and tapped his fingers softly. "When Tad left, this friend dug into Margot's and Tad's finances and found that Tad had opened several credit cards and maxed them all out. The address statements went to a P.O. box in the city they lived in, so Margot never knew about any of it. Our friend also checked Margot's credit and her daughters'. Luckily, he left all of them alone."

"Do you know what he bought? Was there a mistress?" Sorenson asked.

"Not that we know of," Max replied. "The running theory is he possibly had a gambling problem. He made large purchases at electronics and big box stores. We think he was pawning the items for cash to pay off debts."

"But you have no proof of that?" Gallagher asked.

"No."

"I asked them to stop looking," Margot said. "I just wanted to move on. He left us, and I didn't want to expose my daughters to his problems. If he wanted to come back into their lives, he needed to do it whole and problem-free."

"You said he gave up custody, correct?" Sorenson asked.

"Yes."

"Completely?" Sorenson raised a hand and made a quick cutting motion. "Not just visitation, but everything?"

"Yes. The divorce decree was very clear. He gave up any rights to them at all."

"Did you find that unusual for a man who you said loved his children and was a good father?" Gallagher asked.

"Of course I did. But what was I supposed to do? It didn't take long to figure out he didn't want to be found. And honestly, I didn't have the energy to track him down. I had two active toddlers to look after and a career to salvage."

"What's the name of his divorce attorney?" Sorenson asked.

"Ron Peters. He's out of Dallas."

The detective jotted that down. "What about the supervisor you mentioned? And the friends?"

She named them all.

"Is there anyone who would want to hurt your ex-husband?" Gallagher asked.

Margot didn't even need to think. "No. Everyone loved him. I know now there were things about him I didn't know, but he was a good man and well-liked."

The two men shared another look, then Sorenson spoke. "Okay. I think those are all the questions we have for now. Will you be available if we have more?"

"Yes," Max said. "We weren't sure how much time you'd need, so we booked our return flight for Monday. And we can stay longer if necessary, but not too long. Margot's never been away from the twins for more than a work shift. They're in good hands with friends, but—"

Gallagher waved a hand. "Say no more. I have three kids of my own, so I get it. It's hard being away from them. I'm sure Monday will be fine. I think any follow-up questions beyond that can be asked over the phone or through Zoom. Do you have any questions for us?"

"I have one." Max raised a finger. "Do you know how long he's been dead?"

"Best guess from the M.E. is early fall. The cold water really slowed down decomp, but there's some," Sorenson said.

"And his car." Max sat forward, a curious frown pulling down his eyebrows. "You said it was found on federal land." He fixed his gaze on Gallagher. "Where?"

Margot wanted to know that too.

"Out near Medora. A ranger in Theodore Roosevelt National Park found it well off the beaten path."

"Would it be possible for us to look at it? Margot might recognize something. Was he living out of it?" Max leaned forward, folding his hands together on the table.

Gallagher tipped his head, studying Max. "Who are you? I know you said you're her friend, but you talk like an investigator. Not just the questions, but your tone and bearing."

Margot pressed her lips together and eyed Max, wondering what he would say. Probably some semblance of the truth.

She imagined the agent would do a search on him once they left. It wasn't just the nature of Tad's death that caused them to ask her to come here. They'd wanted to assess her as a suspect in his murder. Max had unknowingly put himself on their radar.

A wolfish smile graced Max's face. "Officially? I'm just her friend. But my friends and I, we get... involved in things sometimes that turn us into investigators."

Gallagher's eyebrow shot up. "Are you a lawyer too? Because that was some sort of doublespeak."

Max chuckled. "No. I'm just a business owner."

"And?" The agent rolled a hand. "What am I going to find out about you when I run your name?"

A hardness settled over Max's features, turning his eyes a steely blue. Margot didn't see it often. He was usually good-humored and a bit silly. But when pushed, the warrior side of his personality peeked out. She quite liked that his seriousness lurked underneath his fun-loving personality. Life with Max around was fun, but she knew that when the tables turned, she could count on him.

"I'm former Air Force. And I have some... influential friends."

"Such as?"

"Why does it matter?"

Agent Gallagher lifted a shoulder.

Max stared at him, staying quiet. Margot wondered why Max didn't answer and why the agent wanted to know.

Finally, Gallagher broke the staring contest. He smiled and sat back. "Well, unless either of you have other questions, we're done here."

"You didn't answer mine," Max said. "Can we see Tad's car and its contents?"

Gallagher exchanged another look with Sorenson.

The detective aimed a shrug at the agent. "It's up to you. The car's in your jurisdiction. I don't have a problem with it. He's right. She might find meaning in something we dismissed."

The agent pursed his mouth, then nodded. "All right. How about this afternoon? Around three o'clock? The car's at our facility in Bismarck. I can email directions to Dr. Gaultier."

"That's fine with me," Margot said. She looked at Max, who nodded.

"Great." Gallagher pushed away from the table to stand. "Until this afternoon, then."

Max stood, offering him a tight smile. "Make sure you do your research on me before you come. You know, so you can pepper me with more questions that don't have anything to do with your investigation."

Oh my.

Margot turned away to hide her smile as a deep frown came over Gallagher's face. It probably wasn't wise to bait a federal agent, but Max was right. His background wouldn't help them solve this case.

"I'll do that." Gallagher drummed his fingers once on the folder in front of him, his mouth tight. Picking up his notepad and pen, he spun on his heel and headed for the exit, Sorenson right behind him. They paused at the door and glanced back expectantly.

Max held out a hand to her. Margot took it, letting him help her from the chair, and didn't let go as they walked toward the men.

With a nod, Max led her past them and into the hall. Silence reigned as they were led to the lobby.

Sorenson pushed a button on the wall, and the door buzzed, letting them out. "Have a safe trip to Bismarck."

"Thank you," Margot muttered.

Max pulled her through the doorway. Once outside, he glanced at her. "I guess we're taking a road trip."

"Apparently." She reached for the zipper on her jacket, steeling herself against the icebox they'd walked into. "But we're going coat shopping first."

Eight

Agent Gallagher met them at the door when they arrived at the FBI facility in Bismarck. Minutes after walking through the front doors, they were deep in the bowels of the building and going through a heavy steel door into a large warehouse that housed nothing but cars. Most of them were intact, looking like they were just waiting for someone to come drive them away. But others were chunks of shredded metal and twisted frames. Some were filthy, like they'd been exposed to the elements for an extended period of time. Margot couldn't help but wonder the stories behind some of the cars. What heinous crimes had been committed and who'd been hurt for these vehicles to end up in an FBI warehouse?

The agent wound through the aisles of cars and stopped in front of an older-model black Honda sedan. He held out a hand. "This is it."

Margot tipped her head, studying it. At least it was intact.

The car looked like something Tad would drive. Sensible. Unassuming. Neat. Even though it was old—much older than anything she'd ever seen him drive, including when they were in college—it was well kept.

Max walked toward it, circling the vehicle. He paused near the driver's door and peered down at the windshield.

"Do you recognize it?" Gallagher's gaze traveled between him and Margot.

"No." She moved forward as Max continued his circuit around the vehicle. Looking in the windows, she didn't see much. It was empty of everything that didn't originally come with the car. "Where's all the stuff you said was in it?"

"This way." Gallagher flicked his head to the side, then turned and walked deeper into the maze.

Margot glanced at Max, and they shared a quick look of trepidation before following the man. Nearing the rear of the building, she saw another door. Gallagher walked up to it, entered a code into the keypad on the wall, then led them through into a giant storage room. A long table filled the space directly in front of them. Beyond that and behind a wall of chain link sat rows and rows of metal shelving, each laden with boxes and items in evidence bags.

Gallagher walked up to the fencing and pulled a set of keys from his pocket, unlocking the gate. He stopped on the other side, propping the door open with his foot so he could slide boxes and a suitcase wrapped in plastic wrap and sealed with evidence tape through the opening.

Max stepped forward to pick them up, setting each one on the table. Margot wandered over, hands stuffed in her jacket pockets, and peered inside the white cardboard boxes. They were full of evidence bags. The writing and the haphazard way the items were boxed made it difficult to see what was inside.

The gate clanged shut, then Gallagher walked over. "You can take things out and look. Just don't remove the items from the evidence bags. When you're ready, I'll open the suitcase."

"Got it." Margot reached into the first box, pulling out bag after bag of clothing. She paused as she withdrew a t-shirt. Her lower lip quivered and moisture gathered in her eyes. It was the shirt she'd given Tad for Father's Day last year. She'd painted the girls' hands and feet, then stamped the shirt.

"That shirt mean something to you?"

Gallagher's voice interrupted her thoughts, and she looked up. "Um. Yeah." She cleared her throat. "It's Tad's. These are our daughters' hand and footprints."

"You're sure?"

"Yes. I made the shirt myself last year for Father's Day. It was his first, since they were born just after Father's Day the year before."

"I see they get their love of fingerpainting naturally." Max's dry tone made her smile. She glanced over to see him smiling at her. The teasing light in his eyes told her he was remembering the tile incident from a couple of months ago.

She chuckled. "I've encouraged it, yes."

Putting the shirt down, she dug through the rest of the box. It was mostly more clothes. "Did you take the stuff out of his suitcase?"

Gallagher crossed his arms, tipping his head as he studied her. "No. That was all laying in the backseat. Probably dirty laundry."

A quick pang went through Margot's heart at the thought he'd been wearing the shirt with the twins' prints on it.

Oh, Tad. Why did you leave the girls?

With a quick sniff, she moved on to the next box. It was more of the same, but nothing gave her pause this time. The third box contained non-clothing items the agents found in the car. Receipts, a phone charger, sunglasses, a book, and a postcard.

She frowned as she lifted the latter out of the box. The scene on the front was of a tropical beach. At the bottom, written in fancy script, were the words Costa Rica. A jolt of curiosity zinged through her. "Max."

"What did you find?" He stepped closer.

Agent Gallagher edged closer, too, but hung back.

Margot showed Max the postcard.

His gaze sharpened when he saw the text. "Is there anything written on the back?"

She turned it over. "'The people down here are great. It's a shame you left.' Signed, F." Margot frowned, looking at Gallagher. "Who's F?"

"Don't know. Do you?"

"It's not ringing any bells, no."

"Does Tad have any friends whose name starts with an F?" Max asked.

Margot stared at the postcard, running a list of her ex's closest friends through her mind. After a moment, she shook her head. "Not anyone that I can think of. I'm sure he has colleagues and other people he associated with at work whose names start with that letter, but I can't think of anyone who would send him a postcard."

"Can I see that?" Max held out a hand.

She gave it to him. "What are you thinking?"

"I want to look at the postmark." He let out a soft grunt. "It's from September. And it was sent from Costa Rica."

"That mean something?" Gallagher asked.

"No. Just puzzling things out. Tad wasn't ever in Costa Rica." Max glanced at Margot. "Right?"

"If he was, he didn't visit," she confirmed.

"So, why does it say it's a shame he left?"

Margot blinked, processing that. "I don't know."

"And who was he with? The wording implies he was with someone."

"There's another possibility." Gallagher's quiet voice interrupted their back and forth. They both turned to look at him.

The agent hesitated. A sinking feeling settled into her stomach when she took in the pinch to his expression.

Finally, he spoke. "The note could be in reference to you

and your daughters, Dr. Gaultier. You could be the people, and it could be a shame he left you."

NINE

Max held back a curse at the agent's theory.

It felt spot-on. But the implications of it were not something Max wanted to think about. It meant Margot and the girls were in danger.

"Have you noticed anyone lurking around you lately?" Agent Gallagher asked Margot.

She blinked at him several times, then looked at Max. The wide set to her eyes rang with fear.

A stab of it went through his chest. If this theory held any weight, she and the twins were moving in with him as soon as they returned home.

After a moment, she took a shaky breath and answered the agent. "No. But it's not like I've been looking."

"What about strangers?" Gallagher's gaze bounced between them. "Have there been any of those popping up? Maybe the same person more than once?"

"We live in a tourist destination," Margot answered, raising a hand to whisk a strand of hair behind her ear in a gesture Max recognized as a nervous tell. He edged closer and lightly touched the back of her sleeve, letting her know he was there.

"And I'm in the middle of opening a medical clinic," she continued. "I'm surrounded by strangers every day. But none of them give me the creeps, Agent Gallagher."

The agent turned to Max. "Have you noticed anyone?"

"No." And after all the trouble they'd had lately with everyone else, he'd have picked up on something unusual. They'd all been on alert. But he'd be making a phone call home as soon as they left here. Just to double check that everything was fine, and to make sure everyone stayed on their toes.

"Okay. Well, I wouldn't be too worried about it. But stay vigilant. It's been several months since that was mailed, so it's probably nothing."

Max chewed on the corner of his mouth, a deep vee between his eyebrows. Gallagher made a good point, but it didn't completely allay his fears. He could tell from the tightness on Margot's face she felt the same.

But there was little they could do now without more information. "Let's keep looking, yeah?" He glanced at Margot and nodded to the boxes.

She blew out a long breath. "Okay."

It took another fifteen minutes before she made it through the rest of Tad's things, including the suitcase. She identified a few more items that belonged to him, but there were no more strange notes.

"Do you have Tad's keys?" Max asked as Gallagher wrapped evidence tape around the suitcase.

The agent looked up with a frown. "Why?"

Max lifted a shoulder. "Just being thorough." His hope was maybe there was one on there Margot recognized, or one they could trace. He was also curious why they weren't with the other items.

"They're in my office."

"Is that in this building?"

"It is, yes." Gallagher finished the suitcase and set it on its wheels. "Let's put all these back in the cage and I'll take you up there."

"Sounds good." Max reached for a box.

Between the three of them, it only took a minute to get everything back behind the fencing. With it all locked up, Gallagher led them from the room. Winding back through the maze of cars, they reentered the main building, then took the elevator to the third floor and turned down a long hallway.

Halfway down the corridor, the agent stopped and unlocked a door. Entering, he flipped on the lights, then crossed to the desk.

"Here you go." He scooped up an evidence bag from the desktop and passed it to Max.

Taking the bag, Max turned it over in his hands, examining the keys. "You said these were on the body you pulled from the lake?"

"Yeah. We've run them for prints, but the water erased anything usable."

Max stepped closer to Margot and tipped the bag toward her. "Do you recognize any of the keys?"

She took it from him, peering through the plastic. After a moment, she pointed to one. "That's our house key."

Gallagher's gaze sharpened. "You're sure?"

"Yes. I put that red nail polish on it myself. He could never remember which key it was, so I marked it. I did the same to mine, and to the keys for my new house in Costa Rica."

"She did." Max glanced at the agent. "I've seen her house keys. The tops of both are painted red."

"Do you recognize any of the others, Dr. Gaultier?"

Margot peered through the plastic again, slowly shaking her head. "No. I don't think so. One looks like a bank deposit box key, but I don't know what it would be to. I have a safe deposit box, but Tad never had access to it."

"Why not?"

"It's a family thing. My parents opened it for me when I was born and put a selection of family heirloom pieces in it. I've only ever looked in it once and that was when they gave me the keys when I turned twenty-one. I opened the box, withdrew all the contents and moved it to a bank of my choice."

"What's in it, if you don't mind me asking?"

"Just jewelry and some coins. It's part of my inheritance, but I've never touched it."

"Are these traceable pieces?" Gallagher crossed his arms. "I'll be honest, Dr. Gaultier. I looked you up. I know what kind of background you come from. It surprises me that you don't live a more lavish lifestyle."

"Yes, well, my family's lavish lifestyle meant I had a lonely childhood. And I don't need—or want—my parents' money to provide for my daughters. I vowed the day I opened the box that using its contents would be an absolute last resort."

"You turned your back on your family's wealth?" He raised a skeptical eyebrow.

"Yes. It's never brought anything but loneliness and heartache for me. As for your question about whether the items are traceable, I imagine some of them are, yes."

"Do you have paperwork on them? Provenance or insurance?"

"I do."

"Is there any chance your ex-husband could have accessed the box?"

"I doubt it. Not unless a bank employee took a bribe. I'm the only person authorized to access it."

"And that key isn't one you recognize?" He motioned to the evidence bag in her hands.

She glanced at it again. "No." Margot held it out. "I'm sorry I can't be of more help."

Gallagher took the bag. "You've been plenty helpful. The only other thing I ask is that you consider checking on your safe deposit box."

Margot's forehead wrinkled. She opened her mouth to speak, but the agent held up a hand.

"Just to be thorough."

She snapped her mouth closed, then nodded once. "I'll think about it. The bank is in Texas."

Max made a mental note to change their return flight itinerary. They'd stop in Dallas for a day and go to the bank before heading home. If she didn't have her key, he'd have Dean overnight it to their hotel. He knew from the look on her face she didn't want to go check the box, but he also knew it would bug her if she didn't.

Gallagher set the keys down on his desk and moved toward the door. "Thank you both for coming. I appreciate you making the trek up here. I know the weather isn't the greatest."

"It's definitely tested our tropical blood." Max extended an arm, ushering Margot toward the door as he aimed a one-sided smile at the agent.

"I bet." Gallagher grinned. "To be fair, it's not normally this cold this early. I'm hoping it gets it out of its system now and we have warmer temperatures in January and February."

Max's smile bloomed. "Keep dreaming."

The agent chuckled softly. "I know."

They reached the elevator and rode it back down to the lobby. Gallagher walked with them to the doors.

"Dr. Gaultier, Mr. Carson, thank you for your help." He held out a hand, but his eyes were on Margot. "I know this wasn't easy for you."

Margot's calm expression didn't change except for a slight

tension around her mouth. Max doubted Gallagher saw it. Unless someone knew her well, it wasn't that noticeable.

"Um, could I ask a favor?" She asked the agent.

"What's that?"

"When this is all over, can I have that shirt with the girls' prints on it?" The sadness Max glimpsed when she first saw the shirt returned. He wanted to reach out and hug her, but there was a rigidness to her that told him she didn't want to be touched right now. He had a feeling she was hanging on to her emotions by a hair.

"Of course. I'll make sure it gets to you," Gallagher said.

"Thank you."

"You're welcome. I know I seemed reluctant to have you go through your ex-husband's things earlier today, but your input was valuable."

Max resisted the urge to snort and roll his eyes. All the agent had learned was that the items in the car belonged to Tad and someone had a connection to Costa Rica. The latter was of most interest to Max. He wished he'd been able to take a picture of the barcode on the postcard. Asher might be able to get a post office location from it. He was sure the feds could, but they wouldn't share that information. He also wished he had a picture of that safe deposit box key. He'd memorized the numbers on it, but it would be nice to have a picture of the shape. They weren't all the same. And thanks to a handy mnemonic trick he'd learned in the military, he'd memorized the VIN and the license plate from the car as well. Once they got into the car, he'd write it all down. Later tonight or tomorrow, he'd get the information to Asher.

"I'm glad I could help. You or Detective Sorenson will keep me updated, yes?" Margot asked.

"We'll do our best." Gallagher reached into his pocket and took out a business card. "If you have questions or you think of something that could be useful, please call."

She took the card. "I will. Thank you."

"Thank you for your time." Max extended a hand to the man.

"Yep." Gallagher took it. "Have a safe trip back to Minot."

"We will." Max released the agent's hand, then placed it on Margot's back, ushering her toward the door.

That wintry North Dakota air blasted him in the face as they stepped outside.

"Why do I get the feeling that's the last we'll hear from him until they make an arrest?" Margot asked, tucking her head into the wind as they hurried to the car.

Max snorted softly. "Because it probably is."

Reaching the car, he unlocked it, and they got in, out of the wind. He started the engine. It shouldn't take long for the heat to kick in. They hadn't been inside that long. Taking his phone from his pocket, he jotted down all the information he'd memorized, then put the device away.

"Ready to go?" He glanced over at Margot to make sure she had her seat belt on.

She did, but it was the tense look on her face that made him pause. He leaned forward so he could better see her face. Moisture shimmered in the corner of her eye as she stared out her window.

"Hey." He extended a hand to cover hers. "Are you all right?"

"I'm fine," she quickly shot back, still staring out the window.

"No, you're not. Talk to me, Margot."

"I can't." Her voice stayed low and controlled. "Not right now."

"Margot—"

"Please, Max. Just drive." The controlled tone remained in her voice, but he recognized it for the coping mechanism it was. She was hanging on by a thread.

Clenching his teeth, he sat back. He didn't want to force her to talk; it would just make her angry at him. Her ex-husband was a touchy subject. Pushing her to talk could drive a wedge between them.

Contrary to what the team thought, he wasn't as secure in his relationship with Margot as it appeared. He worried every day she'd come to her senses and realize that a friendship with a single man on the downswing toward fifty wasn't doing her any favors in the romance department and yank the rug out from under him. As much as he wished there could be more with Margot, he wasn't a fool. He knew how old he was compared to her.

But that didn't stop him from wanting more. She and her twin terrors had wormed their way into his heart with little effort. He'd do anything for Margot and the girls.

Right now, that meant he needed to keep his mouth shut and drive.

So, that's what he did.

TEN

The bitter wind swirled Margot's hair around her face, but she didn't feel the bite in the air. Her racing thoughts and rioting emotions chased away any discomfort. She knew she should probably go inside, but it felt safer to deal with her emotions out here, where there was space. She wasn't normally claustrophobic, but the walls of her room had closed in on her shortly after they returned to the hotel. She'd paced the floor for about ten minutes before donning her coat and escaping outside. Now, she was huddled in an alcove at the side of the building, staring at the snow-covered field kitty-corner to the hotel.

Max would likely come looking for her soon. They hadn't eaten dinner yet. When they returned, she'd mumbled something about needing some time to herself, then fled into her room.

It was cowardly, she knew. Especially after the silence on the hour and a half ride back. But she just needed some room to breathe. Somewhere without anyone's eyes on her—no matter how kind or well-meaning.

Part of her wanted to walk into that field and scream. Tad was supposed to be behind her. She'd moved on.

But here he was, invading her thoughts and making her sad again. She'd already mourned the loss of her marriage. But she'd never wished him dead. Deep down, she'd harbored hope he'd figure out whatever was going on with him and come back to be a father to Emily and Lily.

That could never happen now.

A tear trickled down her face, the skin of her cheek growing tight as the moisture froze to it. She didn't bother wiping it away. Another one would just fall. Icicles could form and she wouldn't care.

Darkness gathered around her. Long shadows fell on the ground from the building and the trees. Streetlights blinked on, chasing some of them away.

The temperature dropped as the sun went down, and soon, Margot couldn't feel her nose. But she still couldn't bring her feet to move her body inside. Huddling deeper into her coat, she pulled the hood tighter around her head and tucked her nose in her collar. Her teeth weren't chattering yet. She'd go in when that happened.

A tall figure rounded the corner of the building. Wind whipped through his dark blond hair and fluttered the lapels of his coat as he walked down the sidewalk, hands stuffed into his pockets.

Max.

Margot saw him before he saw her. Without thinking, she stepped back, still wanting to be alone, but stopped herself before she could fully sink into the shadows. He'd raise the roof if he couldn't find her. She imagined he was already concerned, since she wasn't inside. She'd made it no secret it was too cold here for her.

The man was a saint. She didn't know how she'd lucked into finding a friend like him.

She took a moment to study him. Lately, she'd begun to wish for more than friendship. Taking that leap, though—she wasn't sure she could. Not with Max. The thought of losing his friendship if something went wrong scared her to no end. He'd been her rock this past year. He and Annabeth. He regularly swooped in and took some of the burden off her shoulders. Everything from staying with the girls so she could grocery shop in peace to cracking a joke that made her laugh. Somewhere along the line, he'd become a fixture in her life.

But it was getting harder to ignore what his smile did to her insides. Or how his kindness turned her heart to mush. The age gap didn't matter to her. Sure, they had some different early life experiences, but thanks to her lonely childhood, she'd been forced to grow up fast. She'd never felt her age, always older. The calendar said she was thirty-two, but she felt like she shared a worldview with someone closer to forty. Tad was the closest in age she'd ever dated. They were just months apart. But he'd matched her maturity level. Her feelings for a man Max's age weren't out of the realm of what was normal for her.

She didn't know what to do about it. Ignoring it wasn't really an option anymore. Several times in the last month, she'd stopped herself from leaning in to kiss him. One day, she was going to do it without thinking. He'd be leaving or something, and she'd be distracted and would just lean in and give him a quick peck.

It would change everything.

Once more, her gaze traveled over his tall form as he walked closer. He still hadn't seen her.

That coat sure did something for his shoulders. They were already broad, but he looked massive in that jacket. And he had legs to match. Dark denim molded to his solid, thick thighs. They were the legs of someone who worked out daily.

But not to excess. They were just right.

Margot stifled a groan and rolled her eyes. How did she go from mourning her ex to salivating over Max?

It was a sign she needed to see a therapist.

Yeah, right. And you'll work that into your schedule where?

Her inner voice wasn't wrong. She didn't have time for therapy.

Which was probably why she was so upset over today's events. Although, she'd like to think she was upset because, despite what he'd done, she loved Tad, even if she wasn't in love with him anymore. He was her daughters' father. A man she'd pledged to love, who'd pledged to love her.

Just like that, the melancholy was back.

Margot huffed.

Dammit.

Max paused, and she knew he'd heard her.

She stepped out of the alcove.

"There you are." His feet moved again, double-time. "I've been looking everywhere for you."

Margot let out a soft squeak of surprise as he grabbed her, pulling her into his chest for a hug. His palm cradled the back of her head, knocking her hood askew. She clutched the sides of his coat.

Leaning back, he looked at her. "I knocked on your door about forty minutes ago. When you didn't answer, I thought maybe you were napping or in the shower, so I went and got us dinner. Then you still didn't answer. I've been all over the hotel. What are you doing out here? Have you been out here the whole time?"

"Yeah. I needed some space. Not from you," she hastened to add. Raising a hand, she repositioned her hood so she could see his face as she looked up at him. "In my head." She pointed to her temple. "Cold air, staring at a field—it seemed like the best option. I didn't mean to worry you."

He let her go and took her hand. "It's all right. I get it. Come on. Let's go eat. And get you warmed up."

That mushy feeling in her heart returned. There was no judgment or anger in his tone or his words. Just acceptance and forgiveness. She was also thankful he didn't ask questions.

"I'm actually not too cold. Mostly my face. This new coat is great." Her legs were a little chill, though. The denim covering them wasn't as protective as the heavy parka.

"I'm glad. You were out here for a while." Max led her back to the alcove where she'd been hiding. He swiped his key card over the reader by the door and let them inside.

Warmth blasted Margot in the face. A tingle raced through her icy cheeks, and she was acutely aware of her chilled flesh beneath her jeans. Maybe she was colder than she thought.

They walked up the steps just inside the door to their rooms. The trek helped circulate her blood, and an ache started in her thighs.

Yeah. She'd stayed out too long.

"Do you want to eat alone?" Max asked. "It's okay if you do."

Margot's heart flip-flopped. She didn't deserve this man. And she was done wallowing in her anger and grief. It wouldn't help anything.

"Actually, I think I'd like the company."

ELEVEN

Surprise rendered Max speechless momentarily. She wanted to eat with him? He knew she'd seen him long before he saw her. From her vantage point, it would have been impossible not to.

So, what had changed that she no longer wanted to be alone?

He didn't have the answer and wasn't about to look a gift horse in the mouth. "Okay. The food is in my room. Do you want to eat there, or do you want me to bring it to you?"

"Would you mind bringing it to my room? I'd like to put on some sweats. These jeans are chilly."

"Sure. Unlock the connecting door?" He took a step toward his room.

She nodded. "Yep."

Turning away, she went into her room. Max entered his and immediately removed his coat, draping it over the desk chair.

The room smelled divine. He'd found a local place that served just about everything and ordered them each some salmon. They were used to fresh seafood nearly every day. He didn't know about Margot, but he missed it, and they'd only been gone a couple of days.

Removing the to-go boxes from the bag, he opened one to check the temperature. The food had cooled off significantly since he brought it back.

Not a problem. He'd just pop the cardboard cartons in the microwave. Margot needed a few minutes to change, anyway.

Once he'd heated both boxes, he put them back in the bag and opened the connecting door. With a quick rap of his knuckles on hers, he twisted the knob and walked in.

The room was empty.

A quick glance around the corner revealed a closed bathroom door. The light shone through underneath.

"Food's here," he called.

"I'll be out in a second." Her muffled voice came through the door.

Max set the bag on the desk. By the time she emerged from the bathroom, he had the boxes out and was busy opening utensils.

"That smells great. Fish?"

He nodded. "Salmon. I know it's different from what we get at home and not as fresh, but I was craving seafood." He handed her a box and a utensil set.

She took it with a smile and climbed up on the bed to sit cross-legged. Max sat in the desk chair, spinning to face her.

"Have you warmed up?"

"Mostly." She flipped open her to-go box. "Hot food will finish the job. Thank you for getting it."

"Not a problem." He lifted the lid on his own dinner and speared a chunk of fish with a plastic fork. "So, how are the girls? Have you talked to Annabeth?"

Margot shook her head as she swallowed a bite. "She texted me some pictures. I don't think they miss me at all. They were at the beach, sand buckets in hand."

Max grinned. "Did Emily bury Dean?"

Margot laughed, the sound warming Max's insides. "I'm sure she tried. She'd need a substitute with you gone."

He chuckled. "Well, soon enough, she can go back to dumping buckets full of it onto my chest." Seafood wasn't all he missed about home. It still astonished him how much he missed the girls when he wasn't there. In October, when he'd been in the States with Sam and Dean, he'd lived for pictures from Margot.

"You know, I don't think I've ever thanked you for letting me be such a big part of their lives." He tried to keep the statement casual by scooping up a forkful of rice. He didn't want to make things heavy, but he wanted her to know how much he appreciated her and the twins in his life. It was something they never really talked about.

Margot toyed with the food in her box. She cast a quick glance at him through her lashes. "I should be the one thanking you. I don't know what I'd do without you." She looked up, meeting his gaze. "That's the honest truth. I don't know why you want to be friends with a divorced mom of twin toddlers, but I'm grateful."

Max caught his bottom lip between his teeth, glancing away as he slowly let it loose. How did he respond to that without sounding like a pathetic and lonely middle-aged man? She and the twins had filled a void in his life he didn't even know was there until they showed up.

"It's not hard being your friend, Margot. Or loving the girls. They're wonderful. So are you." His heart thumped at the admission. It was the closest he'd ever come to telling her how he really felt.

Color stained her cheeks. "I think you're wonderful too," she said, her voice quiet as she looked up.

Max held her gaze, weighing his next words. It felt like they were at a turning point. He could smile, thank her, and change the subject, keeping their relationship at status quo. Or he could see if she had a willingness to take things to another level.

If he left things as they were, that likely meant he'd lose whatever chance he had at anything more with her. They'd be friends, and only friends. Right now, he could deal with that. But what percolated at the back of his mind was how would he feel if she met someone? What happened to their friendship if she started dating?

It meant he'd lose her and the twins. Because he'd step back and let her boyfriend move into the role he'd been in. She didn't need two men vying for the same duties. It didn't make sense.

In either scenario, he could lose her. But only one offered them both so much more.

So, he took the leap.

He reached over and gently curled a hand over the one holding her to-go box on her lap. "If we both feel that way, what do we do about it?"

A slight rounding to her eyes told him she caught his meaning. Quickly, her gaze dropped. He saw her forehead wrinkle as she pushed her food around with her fork.

"I'm... not sure it's wise for us to do anything about it."

The hesitation in her voice made his heart leap. Whether it was from fear that she really was turning him down or hope that she wasn't, he didn't know. Sucking a breath in through his nose, he laid the rest of his feelings out for her. "Maybe not. But I don't want to lose you, Margot."

Her head snapped up, and a frown marred her smooth forehead. "What? Why would you lose me?"

He lifted a shoulder and gave voice to the thoughts running through his mind. "Not right away, I won't. But down the line? What happens if I don't act and you meet someone? Where does that leave me?"

"I haven't even thought about dating."

"I know. And I'm not saying we have to. I—" He stopped and glanced away, his mouth flattening as he tried to find the words.

Margot pulled her hand away and set her food on the bed, then scooted forward. Her hand landed on his knee. Warmth blossomed in the skin beneath his jeans and spread outward to curl in his belly. He itched to cover her hand and intertwine their fingers, but he didn't dare touch her just yet. Not until he knew where they stood.

"My emotions are all over the place. Before we came here, I thought I was in a pretty good place. I was happy again. My life felt ordered and settled. Finally." Going silent, she looked down at her hand, curling her fingers to scratch at an imperfection in the denim.

Max ignored the part of his brain telling him to wait to touch her. He didn't care if it further complicated his feelings. They were complicated enough, and she looked like she needed some comfort.

"We don't have to talk about it. Not until you're ready." He laid his hand over hers.

"I know." She looked at him then. "But I feel like I owe you an explanation. I mean, I basically gave you the silent treatment, then freaked you out by vanishing into the cold."

"Honey, you don't owe me anything. I know what it's like to need some space. To have your thoughts jumbled up so much that nothing makes sense."

"Still, I... I think I'm ready to talk."

Max set his food on the desk, then moved to the bed. She leaned into him, wrapping an arm through his, and tipped her head into his shoulder.

He kissed the top of her head and waited for her to speak. She could tell him whatever she wanted whenever she wanted. He was just happy she wanted to talk to him.

"It just hit me, you know?" she said, several moments later. "That he's dead and can never come back. Not that I wanted him to. Not for me, anyway. But the girls have lost any chance of ever knowing their father. The man I married and the one who was so excited to be a dad. Not the man who left. My heart hurts for them. For him." Tears formed in her eyes, and she sniffed, glancing away.

Max extracted his arm from her grasp and wrapped it around her shoulders, hugging her close.

"Why did he leave? What drove him away from the two people he loved more than anything? How did he end up—" She broke off with a hiccup.

He wrapped his other arm around her, hugging her tighter. She circled her arms around his waist. He didn't say anything. Reassuring her the police were looking into it and that Tad had his reasons were just empty platitudes that wouldn't help.

They sat there in silence for several minutes. Max stroked her arm and gently rocked as she buried her face in his shoulder and quietly cried, mourning a man she'd once loved and everything that would never be for her daughters.

Resting her cheek on his chest, she peered up at him. "That was a disjointed mess. But I guess what I was getting at is that I was on a path to want more with you."

All the air in Max's lungs stopped moving. He blinked, a slight frown forming. Elation soared through his veins for a moment before her choice of words registered, putting a damper on his feelings.

She said was. Did that mean she wasn't now?

He forced down the lump in his throat so he could speak. "Oh. And now?"

Her hand fluttered over his jaw. "I still do."

TWELVE

Margot had lost her ever-loving mind. What was she doing? Thinking about more with Max and leaning in to kiss him were two wildly different things.

But she'd be damned if she stopped. Hearing him say how he felt—how he wanted more—she couldn't deny it anymore. She wanted this man. Even if getting involved with someone again scared the daylights out of her.

Beard stubble pricked her fingers as she urged his face closer. Those blue eyes that always looked at her and the twins with such kindness now burned a steely blue with desire.

It ignited a fire in her gut. One only he could extinguish.

After he fanned the flames, of course.

Eager to feel the burn, and done playing it safe, she closed the gap.

Holy crap.

The press of his mouth on hers did not disappoint.

White-hot need, more intense than any she'd ever felt, burned through her lips, prickling the skin on her scalp.

Why had she not done this before?

A soft whimper escaped her, which spurred Max's hands into action. He skated one down her arm and over her hip, urging her into his chest. Margot clutched his shirt with one hand, the other still stroking the beard stubble on his jaw.

In just moments, need clawed at her. She wanted this man. Wanted him like she'd never wanted any other before, including Tad. And their sex life hadn't been boring.

But there'd never been this... this... urgency. It consumed her, obliterating all thought except the need to strip them both.

Emboldened by the desire flooding her system, she shifted to straddle his lap.

Max's phone rang from the other room.

With a low groan, he wrenched his mouth away, staring at her with passion-filled eyes for a blink before lifting her up to move her to the side.

"It's Asher."

Margot knew that. She recognized the distinctive ringtone. He was lucky he was hundreds of miles away on the west coast. Where she couldn't reach him to throttle him.

Covering her face as Max hurried through the connecting door, she heaved a sigh. It probably wasn't a bad thing Asher interrupted them. This thing with Max had gone from idle to full speed in an instant. And as good as he made her feel, it was wise for them to take things at a more sedate pace. She valued their friendship and didn't want this to be just a flash in the pan.

That didn't mean her body liked it, though.

Scrubbing her hands down her cheeks, she dropped them into her lap. The low murmur of Max's voice grew louder as he walked into her room. As he stepped over the threshold, he put the phone on speaker. Asher's smooth, rich voice filled the space.

"Hi, Margot."

"Hello, Asher."

"So, I was telling Max, I got a hit on the car."

"That was quick."

"It helped that Max had the VIN and the license plate. It came back registered to a Liam Hughes."

She gasped. "You're sure?"

"Yes. Why?"

"Hughes is my maiden name." She sent a bewildered glance at Max.

"Asher, did you find a driver's license to go with that name?" Max asked.

"Yes. It's a Texas ID, and the picture is definitely Tad. Unless he has an identical twin."

"No. He's an only child. How did he get a driver's license with that name? You need a birth certificate and a social security number."

"There are some great forgers out there," Asher said. "He could have bought a new identity. No need to go through government channels."

"Did you get an address to go with the name?"

"Yeah. It's for an apartment complex in Boise. I did a quick look-up on it. It's one of those short-stay places. He was there for about a month, eight months ago, and there have been two other people registered at the same address since then. It's a dead end."

"Eight months?" Max frowned.

Margot knew her expression looked the same. What happened to the other six?

"I know. That threw me too. Wherever he was for those six months before that, he was completely off the grid. I can't find him. Under his name or this alias. Same goes for after that. There's nothing."

"Okay." Max rubbed his fingers on his forehead. "Did you find anything on the safe deposit key?"

"Not yet. I'll keep looking, but don't hold your breath. There are millions of those things in the U.S. I need more to go on than just the key."

Margot wrinkled her nose. That's what she'd been afraid of.

"All right," Max said. "Keep us posted."

"Yep. You do the same. Talk to you later."

"Bye." Max ended the call and pocketed the phone.

Any desire that had hummed through Margot's veins had disappeared with their conversation. Lusting after Max while discussing her ex-husband's murder felt wrong. She stared at him for several moments, then looked away. Her gaze landed on her shoved-aside dinner, and she picked it up. Toying with her food, she tried to ignore the awkward silence.

Dammit!

Why did she let her hormones take control? Jesus, he probably thought she was a sad sack. A man pays a little bit of attention to her, and she tries to jump his bones. She wouldn't blame him at all if he picked up his dinner and went back to his room.

He moved around the end of the bed and sat on the desk chair.

Margot glanced up in surprise.

"Eat." He motioned to the to-go box in her hands, his gaze soft.

"Max—"

"Eat, Margot. Before your food gets even colder." He speared a chunk of salmon and ate it.

Okay, then. They were pretending nothing happened.

She hoped that didn't go on too long.

Because she couldn't.

That kiss—and what they'd almost done—had upended her world. Saying they wanted more and acting on that were two entirely different things. Talking about it meant things *could* change. Acting on it meant things *had* changed.

And she needed to know where they went from here.

Thirteen

Max stifled a yawn as they got out of the car at Westwood Bank & Trust bright and early Monday morning. On Saturday morning, he'd asked Margot if she happened to have the key to her deposit box on her. To his surprise, she did. It was on her key ring. She kept a spare in her safe at home.

Armed with that information, he'd changed their flight reservations that afternoon, and they'd flown out of Minot on Sunday. They had a flight home at noon today, so here they were at eight a.m. on the dot.

He stifled another yawn as they reached the door. The hour was a respectable one, but he hadn't slept much the last few nights. Too many thoughts of Margot and what they'd almost done running through his mind. Neither of them had the courage to bring up their kiss, despite already acknowledging that they wanted more than friendship. So, they'd continued on like nothing had changed, and he'd lain awake staring at the ceiling, contemplating what life with Margot by his side could look like.

Hushed air enveloped them as they stepped inside the two-story lobby. He always marveled at how a building with marble floors and high ceilings could be so quiet. It must have something to do with the acoustics.

He glanced up. Marble arches soared overhead. Above the teller's desk was a wooden balcony, where he assumed the bank executives had their offices. Cream-colored walls kept the space bright and airy, but did little to muffle the sound of their footsteps on the marble floors. It was a stunning space and lived up to its slightly pretentious name.

Margot walked up to one of the tellers, who greeted them with a smile.

"Hello. How can I help you?" The woman, whose nameplate read "Brittney" asked.

"I need to get into my safe deposit box."

"Of course. Do you have your key?"

"Yes."

"Perfect. I don't have access to that area yet." She gave them a sunny smile. "I'm new. Let me get the manager. If you could meet us over by that door?" She pointed to her right.

"Okay, thank you." Margot backed away and turned.

Max glanced around the nearly empty lobby as they wandered over to the area the teller indicated, noting the lack of other people. There were no other customers yet.

"It's eerie in here," he whispered.

Margot let out a soft chuckle. "Banks always remind me of funeral homes. Quiet and formal, with a hint of secrets behind the scenes."

He snorted. "That's the truth. But places like that—like this"—he twirled a hand—"always make me want to break the rules. When I was a kid, my grandma slapped my hands with her fan at a funeral once because I kept playing with my cousin's braids while the preacher talked."

Margot laughed, the sound echoing through the grand

space. She slapped a hand over her mouth, amusement dancing in her eyes.

Max's low laugh joined hers. "We'd both definitely get a swat if she were here."

"Good thing she's not."

They reached the area near the vault, where the teller had asked them to wait. Margot took his hand and leaned into him, looping her other arm over his.

"You doing okay?" he murmured against her hair. She'd held up fairly well since her breakdown, but he knew grief could hit when it was least expected.

"Yeah. Ready to go home and hug my babies."

Max was too. He missed the little rug rats.

Margot straightened, but didn't let go of his hand as the teller walked up with an older gentleman in a suit who carried an electronic tablet in his hands.

"Hello." He held out a hand. "I'm Andrew Skokar."

"Margot Gaultier." She let go of Max to extend a hand. "Nice to meet you."

"Likewise. Brittney said you'd like to access your safe deposit box."

"Yes."

"Do you have an ID on you, ma'am?"

Digging in her purse, Margot produced her passport. Mr. Skokar examined it, then typed her name into the tablet he carried. It took just moments for him to verify her identity. "Very good." He handed her the passport book. "If you'd like to follow me?" He motioned them toward the thick, steel vault door.

Margot tucked her passport into her purse and trailed behind him into the vault. Max hung back a bit with Brittney, not wanting to get in the way.

"Box 1538, correct?"

"Yes."

Producing a set of keys from his pocket, Mr. Skokar walked down the row until he found hers, then unlocked it. Margot took her key ring from her bag and put her box key in the second lock and turned it. The door swung open a fraction. She removed her key and stepped back so the manager could take the box out of its cubby.

With a soft metallic swish, the box came free.

"Let's go into one of our private viewing rooms." He tipped his head toward the vault door.

Margot reversed directions, then they all followed Brittney down a short hall to a small room with a table and a couple of chairs.

Mr. Skokar set the box on the table. "Take all the time you need. When you're finished, please come find me or one of the staff."

"Thank you." Margot offered him a polite smile.

"You're welcome." Bowing slightly at the waist, he left with Brittney, closing the door behind them.

"So, do you remember everything that's supposed to be in there?" Max pointed at the box.

Margot blew out a breath and sat down. "Mostly. We might need to call Annabeth, though, and have her get into my safe. It has the list of the contents."

He pulled out the chair beside her and sank into it. "Let's see what we've got."

She flipped open the lid.

Max let out a low whistle as he got his first glimpse of the contents. "Damn. These are some—" He broke off and shook his head. "Your parents gave you some nice stuff." Just on top, he could see a diamond pendant that was probably ten carats. It hung on a platinum chain. Beside it was a sapphire and diamond bracelet. Pops of ruby red and emerald green shone in the overhead light. He saw some yellow topaz too.

"Yeah. It's pretty, but I really don't want their money.

When I say they didn't really want me, I'm not kidding. I had nannies from day one, and they left me with them frequently to go on all sorts of overseas trips. Even when they were home, I rarely saw them." She picked up a sapphire and diamond bracelet, running her thumb over one of the stones.

"It just makes me feel dirty to have all this, you know? Like I'm just an employee or something they can throw money at to pacify. I'm glad now I never got rid of it, though. One day, I'll divide it up amongst my kids. But until then, it can sit right here and gather dust." She dropped the bracelet back into the box.

He reached in and picked up a coin on a velvet pad. "I've put some of my wealth in hard currency. Gold. Silver. But not rare coins or jewelry. It's a good idea." It was definitely something to consider. He was always looking for ways to diversify his holdings and to have more tangible assets. Stocks were great. Until the market crashed.

"I know some people who could help you with that. I've taken small amounts from my savings over the years and done the same thing. I brought those holdings down to Costa Rica with me."

He glanced at her. "You did?"

She nodded, not looking up from combing through the box. "I have a few pieces of jewelry and some coins. They're all at the house. I wear the jewelry from time to time."

His brow furrowed, then his expression cleared. "The comb you like to wear. And that mother's necklace."

"Yep. I have a ring and a bracelet too. It's not much, but I know it's an investment that I can sell on a rainy day if I need to. I almost did when Tad left."

"I'm surprised he didn't take it and sell it. It would be easy money if he were gambling."

Her hands stilled, then she looked up with wide eyes.

"What?" He frowned. "What did you remember?"

"I'm not sure. He came out of our bedroom once as I was coming out of the girls' room, looking... just... nervous? Jumpy? I didn't think too much of it." She huffed and waved a hand. "But nothing's missing that I can tell."

"Maybe he switched out the stones for fakes. When we get back, we'll find a jeweler and have your stuff checked."

She let out a soft growl. "He better not have. He knew what that stuff was for."

"Maybe to him it was a rainy day."

Her gaze shot to his, fire blazing in her eyes.

He held up his hands. "I'm not making excuses for him. Just giving another perspective."

Some of the starch left her shoulders, and she dug into the box again. "I know. I just wish I knew what he was thinking. What his reasons were for—" She stopped abruptly, her hands stilling. "What in the world?" She pulled a pocket journal from beneath a tray of coins.

"What's that?"

"I don't know."

"It's not supposed to be in there?"

"No. I've never seen it before." She opened the cover.

Max peered over her shoulder. "It's a ledger."

"Of what?"

"Looks like business transactions." A thought hit him, and he uttered a soft curse. "It could be bets. Money owed, and to whom."

With round eyes, she glanced at the pages, turning a few. "This isn't Tad's handwriting."

"You're sure?"

"One hundred percent." Margot looked up. "I went through medical school with the man and lived with him for almost seven years."

"Okay. Put it down. It could belong to his bookie or even another gambler."

She set it on the table. "What do we do with it?"

"I'm going to run to the drugstore I saw on the corner and get some disposable gloves. Then we're going to photograph every page before we call Agent Gallagher. Asher can feed it all into an algorithm similar to what he built for Sam and Audra. Maybe we'll get lucky and get some info. While I'm gone, check the rest of the box. See if there's anything else in there that shouldn't be. Maybe call Annabeth and have her get the content list?"

Margot sent a discomfited look his way, then scooted closer to the table. "You should probably alter our travel plans for the day too. I don't think we're going home."

Fourteen

Margot blinked back tears as Max left. She desperately needed to see her girls, but it looked like it would be at least another day. Probably two. What they'd found—they needed to get it to the authorities in North Dakota.

Swiping at her face, she steeled herself. These tears wouldn't help her do what needed to be done.

Instead of just pushing things around inside the box, Margot began removing items, spreading them out on the table. Bracelets, necklaces, heavy rings—it all went on the table. She laid out the trays of coins side-by-side. Under the last tray was another key. It looked like the safe deposit box key in Tad's belongings. But this one had a keychain.

For a bank.

And not the one she was sitting in.

Heart beating a tattoo in her chest, she left it where it was, not wanting to touch it until Max brought gloves. What had Tad put in that box, and why would he leave her the key?

She let out a soft groan and raked her hands into her hair, briefly grasping the golden strands. What was going on?

Heaving a sigh, she turned her gaze away from the key to

focus on the items strewn over the table. Nothing looked amiss, but it had been a decade since she'd looked at any of it.

Time to call Annabeth.

Finding her phone, she called her friend.

"Hey!" Annabeth's cheery voice picked up on the second ring. "Are you headed to the airport? It's a little early for that, isn't it? Your flight's at noon, right?"

"It is, but that's all changing. We're still at the bank."

"Oh, man. He took it all, didn't he?"

"No. He added things."

"What?" Confusion colored her tone. "Like what?"

"A journal and a key. Max left to get some gloves so we can look through the notebook. But that's not why I'm calling. Can you get in my safe and get the list of things in my safe deposit box?"

"Sure. Let me tell Dean where I'm going."

Margot heard Annabeth moving around. She spoke to her husband, then the door opened and closed as she walked out her back door to cross the short expanse to Margot's house.

Another door opened and closed.

"Okay. I'm here. Where is it?"

"In my closet. Left-hand corner."

It only took a few moments for Annabeth to move through Margot's small house and open the closet door. In seconds, Margot heard the click of hangers sliding over the bar.

"What's the code?"

Margot told her, then heard beeps as Annabeth input the numbers.

"All right, I'm in. What am I looking for?"

"There's a file labeled 'Safe Deposit M and D'."

A short pause came over the line.

"Oh, there it is." Annabeth blew out a breath that sounded like she was clearing hair out of her eyes. "You said the item list, right?"

"Yeah. We need to go through it. Or you can send me a picture to compare."

"I'll do both. We can go through it together; it'll be faster if I read stuff off. Then I'll text it to you, so you have it for whatever."

"Sounds good."

"You ready?"

"Yep." She put the phone on speaker and set it down.

"Emerald and diamond necklace. Gold. Leaf shape. Total weight twelve carats."

Margot stood up as she found it and moved it to the other side of the table. "Got it. What's next?"

For the next ten minutes, they went through the list. Margot shuffled items around, and they got through all the jewelry and a few coins before Max reappeared.

"That Annabeth?" He mouthed.

Margot nodded.

"1982 D Small Date Copper Alloy Lincoln Cent," Annabeth read from the list.

Pointing a finger at the coins, Margot scanned the text on the cardboard surrounds. "Found it." She plucked it from the tray and set it with the others they'd already been through.

Max set the sack he carried on the table and sat down. Plastic rustled as he dug into the bag.

"What's that?" Annabeth asked.

"It's me." Max tore open the package of gloves.

"What else did you buy?" A curious frown wrinkled Margot's forehead.

"Ziploc bags. We can take a few pieces of your jewelry to get them appraised. And I want to preserve any evidence on the journal before we turn it over to the authorities. Did you find anything else while I was gone?"

Margot tipped a finger toward the metal box. "A safe deposit box key for another bank."

His gaze sharpened. He turned to the box and used a gloved hand to lift it out. "It's the same number as the one from Tad's keychain."

"Seriously?"

He nodded. "Do you recognize this bank?"

"Yeah. There are several in the area."

He set the key back in the box. "We'll go there next, I guess." He waved a hand at the stuff spread over the table. "Continue your inventory. I'm going to look through this journal and take pictures." Extending an arm, he picked up the notebook.

"Did you change our flight?"

"Yeah. I just canceled it. I don't know how long we'll have to stay. Gallagher will probably send an agent from the field office here to collect things, but we may have to stay a day or two for questions."

Margot's mouth twisted. She knew that was the case, but secretly she'd been hoping he'd say differently.

"Annabeth, are you and Dean all right with the girls for a couple more days?" she asked.

"Of course we are. They're being angels."

Max snorted. "I highly doubt that. Lily, maybe. But I'm guessing you've rescued Emily from atop a chair or table at least once."

Annabeth's low chuckle came over the line. "Possibly. There's also the possibility I piled pillows on the floor and told her to have at it."

Margot groaned. "She'll be unstoppable when I get back."

"Then she's your problem."

"I love you. So much." Wrinkling her nose, amusement crinkled the corners of Margot's eyes.

Annabeth laughed. "I know. Let's get back to this list now, shall we?"

With a dramatic sigh, Margot sent Max a grin. "Sure."

It took another fifteen minutes to go through all the coins. Just two were missing.

Margot rubbed her forehead and picked up the phone. "Can you find the provenance for those two coins in the folder and send me pictures?"

"Yep. I'll send this list too."

"Sounds good. You might have to scan and email it later."

"I'll just do that now. My printer is one of those three-in-one things."

"That works. Thanks, Annabeth. Give the girls kisses for me?" Her voice grew thick. She missed her babies so much.

"I will. Bye."

"Bye."

Max chimed in his own farewell, then Annabeth hung up.

Margot set the phone down and pressed the heels of her hands to her eyes with a groan. "I just want to go home."

Max's hand landed on her back, rubbing small circles. "I know. So do I. And we'll get there. At least you're not stuck here alone."

She turned her head to give him a soft smile. "No. I'm glad you forced your way onto this trip. For many reasons." Memories of their kiss Friday evening assailed her. She felt her cheeks flush, but didn't look away. They hadn't talked about it, but there'd been a shift in the way they interacted. Touches lingered a little longer and seemed to come more freely; undercurrents of need passed when they looked at each other. It was subtle, but it was there.

His eyes heated, but the rest of his expression stayed neutral.

"So, did you photograph the whole book?" She gestured to the journal.

"I did. I've been looking at the entries too."

"Oh?"

"It's definitely a betting book." He opened it and explained what he saw.

"How do you know this?" She frowned, settling an uneasy look on him. "You don't gamble, too, do you?"

"No. But I spent enough time around guys in the military who did to know the lingo."

"Can you tell what they were betting on?"

"It looks like horses."

"Horses? When you guys mentioned gambling, I envisioned casinos and blackjack tables. Not horse races."

Max lifted a shoulder. "He could have been playing cards too. But this looks like race betting to me."

She blew out a sigh and ran a hand through her hair. "So, what do we do now? We need to check out that other safe deposit box, don't we?"

"Yeah. I'm hoping Tad authorized you to get into the box and didn't just list you or the twins as beneficiaries. If the latter is the case, we'll have to wait for the DNA results to come back and for the M.E. to issue a death certificate. Or see if Gallagher can get a warrant to get into it."

"Can we ask to be there when he opens it?"

"We can, but that doesn't mean he'll let us. But for now, we're going to put all this away, except for a couple pieces of your jewelry and the items Tad added, then we'll go see if we can get into the box." He reached for the drugstore sack and took out the box of Ziploc bags.

"Which of these do you want?" She gestured to the array of jewelry on the table.

Max stood, tearing open the cardboard box. Leaning forward, he perused the pieces. "That one, that one, and that one." He pointed to the emerald necklace, the diamond pendant, and a sapphire and diamond ring.

Margot picked them up and deposited them into the baggie he held open.

"Here." He handed her another bag, then picked up the keychain and put it inside. "We're taking this stuff with us. Someone let Tad into your box. I don't want that same someone removing what was added." He opened another bag and slid the journal inside.

Her eyes rounded. "Do you really think they would? Why? I mean, what would they gain?"

"I don't know. But we're not taking any chances."

She liked his logic. This could be the key to solving Tad's death. So, without a second thought, she stuffed the three bags into her purse, then helped Max put the remaining items back into the box.

"I'll go get the manager." Max took a step back from the table. "Can you put the gloves and bags in your purse?"

"Sure."

He took off the blue gloves he wore and shoved them into his pocket as he headed for the door. Margot picked up the sack, but then had a thought.

"Max."

He paused in the doorway and turned.

"What do we say about this box? Someone let Tad into it and shouldn't have."

Max drummed his fingers on his leg for a moment. "I think nothing for now. Let's find out what's in the other box, then contact Gallagher. And my attorney. This stuff is in your possession and shouldn't be. We—you—need representation."

Her shoulders drooped, but she didn't argue. He was right.

If it weren't for the fact Tad was already dead, she'd wring his neck.

Fifteen

Traffic noise swirled around them on the cool wind in downtown Dallas as they walked the few blocks to the bank listed on Tad's keychain. Max spotted the drugstore where he'd bought the gloves and the Ziploc bags and had a thought. Grabbing Margot's hand, he steered her toward the store's entrance.

"What are we doing?"

"We need to preserve the prints on that key." The doors swished open, and they stepped inside.

"Oh. How?"

"Makeup and packing tape."

"Makeup and—" She sighed. "Max, maybe we should call Gallagher now. If we lift the prints, they won't hold up in court."

He paused near a rack of Maybelline foundation. "Hell." He pinched the bridge of his nose. "I really don't want the cops involved until we know what's in that box."

"I don't, either. But I don't think we have a choice. What if there are prints on it and they belong to Tad's murderer?

What if it's the only connection to the guy, and we blow it because we wanted to play Miss Marple?"

Max sighed. She was right. "Fine." Turning around, he led them out of the store.

"So, where to?"

He paused, thinking. "We could go to the FBI offices here."

"Okay. Where is it?" Taking out her phone, she looked up the address and mapped it. "I think we'll have to take an Uber. The closest DART station to the building is an hour walk."

Max looked down the street, another possibility churning through his brain. "Or, we could see if we can get an agent to meet us at the bank." He glanced back at Margot. "We might have better luck getting the feds to let us see what's in the box if we're already there. Especially if you've got access to it."

"I like that idea."

A passerby bumped Max's arm. They were in the middle of the sidewalk. Tugging on Margot's sleeve, he tipped his head. "Let's stand over here out of the way." They moved under the store's awning and leaned against the building.

"Do you have Gallagher's card on you?"

"Uh, yeah. It's in my bag." She slipped her phone into her coat pocket, then raised her arm slightly, dipping her hand inside.

A furrow formed between Max's brows. "How do you find anything in there? It's like one of those magician's bags. Or Santa's present sack."

Margot laughed. "It is not."

"Yes, it is. You're looking for a two-by-three square of cardboard in that giant thing."

Chuckling, she rolled her eyes, continuing to dig. "You just don't know how to use the magic." In seconds, she held the white rectangle between her fingers under his nose.

Mouth pursed, he plucked it from her fingers. "Thank you."

"You're welcome." She settled the straps over her shoulder with a wide smile.

Max lifted his phone and called the cell number on the card. "He better answer." Putting the phone to his ear, he waited. It rang three times, then the agent picked up.

"This is Agent Gallagher."

"Gallagher, it's Max Carson. Margot and I have some information for you."

"What kind of information?"

"The kind that requires law enforcement to take physical possession of it. We're in Dallas about ready to head into a bank with a safe deposit box key. Can you send an agent to meet us?"

"A safe deposit box key? Is that what you want to turn over? Or is it the contents of the box?"

"Probably both. We think it's Tad's. We did what you suggested and checked on Margot's safe deposit box. This key was inside. I think it's the spare to the one you found on the body. The numbers are the same."

"You're sure?"

"Yes. And there's more. We found a betting journal, and two of her coins are missing."

"Crap on a cracker." The agent sighed. "Okay. Give me the address of the bank. I'll get someone there ASAP."

Max passed along the bank's address. "Can you give us an hour? We have another stop to make."

"Where?"

"Just... somewhere. If it pans out, we'll let your colleague know."

"Mr. Carson, if this is pertinent to my investigation, I need to know."

"That's the thing. I don't know if it is. But don't worry.

If it matters, we'll make sure to pass along the information. Text me the name of the agent, so I know who we're meeting."

A beat of silence passed, then, "Fine. But you better not withhold anything."

"We won't." Mentally, Max crossed his fingers. "Bye." He hung up.

"What other stop do we need to make?" Margot asked the moment he ended the call.

"That jeweler." Max tipped his phone toward the high-end jewelry shop across the street.

Margot's gaze swung that way, then she nodded. "Let's go."

Traipsing to the corner, they waited for the light to change, then walked across the busy street. Max grabbed the golden handle on the glass door and pulled.

Vanilla-scented air wafted into his face as they stepped inside. Plush cream carpet quieted their footfalls and light gleamed from the gold and crystal chandeliers shining on the glass jewelry cases.

"Good morning. How may I be of assistance?"

An older gentleman in a gray suit and light blue striped tie walked around the counter to greet them.

"We're wondering if you could do an appraisal for us? I'm happy to pay you, if you charge for the service." Max returned the man's polite smile.

"If it's for an insurance report, there's a small fee. But if it's just a general inquiry, I'm happy to take a quick look."

"It's the latter." Margot drew her bag down off her arm.

"Let's come over here." Turning, the man led them over to the jewelry cases, moving behind them again. While Margot found the jewelry, the man spread a velvet cloth over the counter and opened a small box that contained a jeweler's loupe.

"My name's Karl, by the way." He offered them a kind smile.

"It's nice to meet you, Karl. I'm Margot." She laid the jewelry on the counter. "This is Max."

"Nice to meet you too." His expression sobered, then turned curious as he took in the jewelry. "These are lovely. Where did you get them?"

"They're mine. Family heirlooms."

Karl picked up the diamond pendant. "Are you looking to sell?"

"No." Margot glanced up at Max.

He could see by the slight wrinkle to her forehead she was unsure what to tell the man.

Max went with a partial truth. "There's some speculation that the stones aren't real. We're just checking."

"Ah. Understandable. I see that all the time. This, I'm pretty sure is real. The clarity is stunning." He picked up the loupe and held it to his eye, then raised the diamond to look at it.

"Yes, this is definitely real. And quite good quality." He set the piece on the cloth, then reached for the emerald necklace.

A soft grunt left the man's throat.

"It's fake, isn't it?" Margot glanced at Max.

His mouth flattened. This was what he'd been afraid of. If one piece was fake, how many more were?

"I'm afraid so, yes. It's a good quality fake, though." Karl looked up. "I'm sorry."

"Not your fault." Max leaned on a hand. "What about the ring?"

Setting the necklace down, he picked up the ring. A moment later, he hummed. "That's interesting." He straightened. "The diamonds are real, but the sapphire isn't."

"Why would the sapphire get replaced, but not the diamonds? There's what, a carat or two in diamonds there?"

The jeweler nodded. "And I'm not sure. Some families will only replace stones as needed. It's possible they only sold the stones they needed to."

Max tucked his tongue into his cheek, thinking about all the jewelry they'd left in the safe deposit box. He glanced at Margot. "I picked these because something about them didn't look right. The pendant tells me I didn't know what I was talking about. We need to get the rest assessed."

Lips flattening, she nodded.

"Sir." Max turned to Karl. "If we brought you more items in a few hours and came back with a federal agent, would you look through them for us?"

Karl's eyes widened. "A federal agent?"

"It's complicated, but yes. We'd really appreciate your help."

The man's gaze traveled between them, then flicked down to the jewelry. He sighed. "All right."

A surge of victory at this small win had Max smiling. He extended a hand. "Thank you."

Karl shook it. "You're welcome. How many pieces of jewelry are we talking?"

"About twenty items total," Margot said. "But many have multiple stones, like the ring."

Karl nodded. "Okay. Do you have documentation on the jewels? So I can compare the quality?"

"On some, yes. I'll make sure to bring that." She picked up the items and put them in her purse.

"Thank you. I'll see you in a few hours, then."

Sixteen

"There. Is that him?" Margot nodded toward the door at a man in a tired gray suit under a bland khaki trench coat. She and Max were seated in a small lounge area at Ranchero Mutual, waiting for Gallagher's colleague to arrive. They'd already told a teller they were waiting on someone. The woman kept sending suspicious looks their way.

The wind that followed the man in fluttered the front of his coat, revealing the badge clipped to his hip.

"I'd say so." Max stood. "That or the teller finally called the cops."

Margot sighed as she stood up. That would not surprise her. Not with their luck.

"Dr. Gaultier? Mr. Carson?" The man walked closer with a curious frown.

"That's us." Max held out a hand. "Agent Dye?"

The man shook his hand. "Yes. Call me Jeremiah." He extended his hand to Margot.

"Nice to meet you," she said.

"Agent Gallagher gave me a quick rundown of this case. Have you opened the box here?"

Margot shared a look with Max, then shook her head.

"No," Max said. "We wanted to, but we didn't want to obscure any fingerprints on the key."

"You'd have done that by picking it up."

"Not if we wore gloves and were extra careful taking it out of the box." Max pulled a fresh pair from his pocket. "We thought about fingerprinting it, but didn't want to tamper with evidence."

Dye raised an eyebrow, and Max's mouth took on a sardonic tilt. "Anymore than we already have. We also figured the staff here might get suspicious if we pulled these babies out to turn our key in the lock." He shook the gloves.

"You'd be right." The man scratched at his temple and blew out a breath. "Okay. You have the key?"

Margot reached into her purse and pulled out the Ziploc bag containing it.

"Perfect." He took the bag, looking toward a counter that ran along the wall to the right. "Let's go see if I can lift any prints from it, then we'll find the manager."

He led them over to the counter and set the bag down. From one pocket of his trench, he withdrew a small black case and opened it, taking out a fluffy brush, a container of black powder, and several fingerprint cards.

It only took him a minute to dust both sides of the key. He found a thumbprint on one side.

"That's a decent print." Covering it with clear tape, he picked it up, looking at it. "I'll run it when I get back to the office." Putting his kit away, he brushed the powder off the counter and picked up the key. "Shall we?" He nodded toward the teller.

Max turned and motioned Dye to go ahead. As the agent walked past, Margot slipped her hand into Max's, and they followed.

The same teller who'd been staring at them suspiciously while they waited looked even more wary as they approached.

Dye lifted his badge from his belt and showed it to her. "Hello. I'm Agent Dye with the FBI. I'd like to speak to your manager, please."

Her eyes widened, then her gaze shot past him to Max and Margot. "Um, sure." She turned her head, looking down the long desk at a woman in a black pencil skirt and a floral patterned black and white blouse, who'd just emerged from the back. In her late forties, the woman had her light brown hair pulled up into a loose French twist. Gold-framed glasses sat on the end of her nose as she stared down at a pile of papers in her hand.

"Tess."

The woman looked up. Her brows pinched as she took in the teller's wide-eyed look and the three people standing on the other side of the desk. A wariness crept into her eyes.

Margot didn't blame her. It probably looked like she was getting robbed.

Dye held up his badge. "Are you the manager?"

She nodded and walked closer. "I am. How may I help you?"

"I'm Agent Dye, FBI. This is Dr. Gaultier and Mr. Carson. We need your assistance getting into a safe deposit box."

"Do you have a warrant?"

"He doesn't," Margot said. "But I have a key. It's a long story, but I'm hoping my name is on the list of people authorized to access the box."

Tess set her papers down and moved to a computer. "May I see your ID, please?"

Digging out her passport, Margot handed it over.

"What's the box number?"

"Two-eighty," Max replied.

The woman's bright pink nails clacked over the keyboard. "Good news." She glanced up with a smile. "You are."

"That's great. We'd like to see the contents," Agent Dye said.

"That's up to Dr. Gaultier." Tess nodded to Margot.

"It's fine. They're here to help."

"Then let's go get you access." She pushed away from the counter, then went through a door set into the wall to her right and came out into the lobby. "Follow me."

Beige carpet turned their footfalls to soft thumps as they went down a hallway. Tess paused outside of a room and opened the door, turning on the light. "You gentlemen can wait in here while I take Dr. Gaultier in to get the box."

"I'm sorry. I need to keep eyes on it," Agent Dye said. "It's part of a homicide investigation."

Tess's eyes bugged. "Oh. Well, then, I suppose you can stand in the doorway. It's a small space."

"That's fine. So long as I can see."

"I'll stay here." Max moved into the room.

A spate of nerves traveled down Margot's spine as they walked away. It wasn't logical. He was only a few feet away. But she'd feel better with him by her side.

"All right, let's see..." Tess entered the safe deposit box vault and walked along the wall of metal doors. Margot trailed behind while Agent Dye stayed in the doorway.

"Box 280 is... here." Tess stopped and inserted her key into a lock.

Margot put on a set of gloves from her purse, then took the key from the bag and stepped up to slide it into the second lock. The door opened, and she let the manager take the box out. Margot pushed the door closed and removed the key, putting it back in the baggie. Whatever was in that box better mean something and not be some wild goose chase.

Back in the room where Max waited, Tess set the box on

the table. "I'll leave you to it. Do you need anything else at the moment?"

"No, I think we're fine, thank you." Agent Dye moved closer to the table.

"You're welcome. Please come ask for me when you're finished."

"We will." He gave her a short nod, and she left, closing the door.

"Let's have a seat, shall we?" Agent Dye motioned to the chairs arranged around the table.

Max pulled one out for Margot, facing the agent. She sent a soft smile at him as she sat, then took his hand as he sank down next to her.

Dye took off his coat and draped it over the fourth chair, then smoothed his tie and sat. "Agent Gallagher asked me to loop him in when we opened this, so I'm going to call him, if that's all right?"

Margot nodded.

"We'd prefer it," Max said. "So we don't have to go over things twice."

The agent made the call. Gallagher picked up almost immediately.

"You're on speaker, Mark," Dye said.

"Good. Hello, Dr. Gaultier. Mr. Carson."

They chimed in with hellos.

"Start from the beginning. You went down to Dallas to look in your safe deposit box and you found a key and a notebook added and two coins missing, right?"

"Yes," Margot said.

"You're sure that's all that's missing?"

"On the surface, yes," Max said. "Margot called a friend who was able to access the list of items stored in the box. They went through it all and only the coins were gone. But the stop

I mentioned?" He paused, giving the agent a moment to connect the dots.

"Yes?"

"We went to a jeweler's on our way here with a couple of the pieces from Margot's collection. Some of the stones have been replaced."

There was a short pause while Gallagher processed that information. "Dr. Gaultier, did your husband know what was in the deposit box? The exact items, I mean?"

Margot bit the corner of her lip, thinking. "I mean, it's possible. I kept the documents in our home safe. He had access to that. Why?"

"Because I'm trying to figure out if he had the reproductions made first and switched things out when he put the journal and the key in, or if he made more than one trip."

"More than one," Max interjected. "The ring the jeweler looked at had the center stone replaced, but the diamonds were real. Tad couldn't have replaced that stone in the bank. A jeweler would need to do that. He'd have taken the ring, had the stone replaced, then brought it back."

"But remember, he asked us if I could get the original appraisal report so he could compare them." Margot held up a finger. "It's possible that one had been tampered with long before I even took possession of it."

Max tipped his head. "That's true."

"So, short answer, we still don't know," Gallagher said. "Okay. What about the journal? Mr. Carson, you said it looked like a betting journal?"

"Yes. My best guess is for horse races. Margot said it's not Tad's writing, though. We don't know who it belongs to. There are no names anywhere."

"All right. Make sure you turn that over to Agent Dye. Our racketeering division can take a look at it. Maybe they can figure out what it all means."

Margot squeezed Max's hand and kept her expression neutral. She was glad he'd photographed the whole thing. Asher would probably work faster. Plus, they'd actually get to know the results.

"We will," Max said. "That and the key. We need to go back to the other bank after we're done here to get the rest of the jewelry. Before we left the jeweler's, we made arrangements to have the remainder looked at."

"I'll come with you." Agent Dye's head bobbed once.

"Sounds good. Open that box now. Let's find out what the other Dr. Gaultier left behind," Gallagher said.

Margot glanced at Max, the hand tucked into his getting slick with nerves. There could be just about anything in there.

He squeezed her fingers. "Do you want me to do it?"

She blew out a breath, ruffling her bangs. "No."

Untangling their hands, she swiped them on her pants, then raised one and lifted the lid.

Her brow furrowed as she looked inside. "A map?"

SEVENTEEN

This mystery just kept getting weirder.

What kind of game was Tad Gaultier playing?

Max stood, taking the gloves from his pocket. Flexing his hands as he put them on, he studied what he could see of the map. He just hoped the game was finished.

Agent Dye donned gloves, too, and leaned over as Max lifted it out, spreading it over the table.

"What's it a map of?" Gallagher asked. "Dye, put me on FaceTime."

While Dye worked on that, Max read the description. "It's a Cass County map."

"What?" Gallagher's face appeared on Dye's phone screen. "Cass County, North Dakota?"

"No. Texas."

"God, this doesn't make any sense." Margot leaned her hands on the table. She glanced up at Max and Dye. "Why would he put a map of some place close to here in a safe deposit box but end up dead in North Dakota?"

"When was that deposit box opened?" Gallagher asked.

"That's a good question," Dye said. He caught Max's eye. "Could you go get the manager?"

Max didn't want to be the lackey, but he knew the agent needed to maintain chain of custody on the map, so he nodded. "I'll be right back."

Stepping out, he hurried down the hall. Tess was behind the desk, staring at the sheaf of papers she'd first appeared with. "Ma'am?"

She looked up with a smile. "Are you all finished?"

"Not quite. Could you bring a laptop and come down to the room?"

Her smile turned around. "Sure. I'll meet you down there."

"Great, thank you."

"Not a problem."

Max turned on his heel. His long legs ate up the carpet. Margot could handle herself, he knew. But this whole thing had thrown her for a loop, and he'd noticed she seemed calmer with him around. If he were in her shoes, he'd probably feel the same way. It was easier to keep it together when you had someone else to share the burden.

When he walked in the room, Margot was pointing at the map.

"What did you find?" He stepped up next to her.

"Tad circled something. An area in the middle of nowhere."

Frowning, Max studied the spot, then took out his phone. "Let's see what's there."

Margot grinned, shaking her head. "You're thinking like —" She broke off, rolling her lips in.

"Yeah." He smirked, catching her meaning as she stopped short of mentioning Asher's name. "He's not the only one with a big brain."

Dye's forehead furrowed, but he didn't ask them to explain. Max was glad. He didn't intend to.

"All right. In that area, there is... not much, honestly." He found the roads surrounding the circled area and zoomed in. "It looks like there might be a farm. I see a house and a couple of outbuildings."

"Put a pin in it and tell me the address, please," Gallagher said.

Max tapped the screen, then read off the address.

The door opened, admitting the bank manager. She froze in the doorway as they all turned to look at her.

Through saucer-like eyes, she stared back, then smiled. "My presence was requested. How can I help?"

It was Agent Dye who spoke. "Can you tell us when Dr. Gaultier opened the safe deposit box?"

A confused frown creased her forehead. She looked at Margot. "You don't remember when you opened it?"

"I didn't. My ex-husband is also Dr. Gaultier."

The woman's frown deepened. "You're the only Gaultier listed."

"That doesn't make sense." Max shot a quick glance at Margot, who looked equally confused.

He turned back to Tess. "Who else is listed?"

She turned her laptop around. "Just someone named Liam Hughes."

"What?" Max frowned. There was that name again. He glanced at Margot. Her round eyes told him she recognized it as well.

"You know something." Dye pointed first at Max, then Margot.

Not wanting to expose Asher or the fact that they'd been investigating behind the FBI's back, Max quickly answered. "Hughes is Margot's maiden name."

"Did he take your name after you married?" Dye aimed his question at Margot.

"No."

Frowning, he turned to the bank manager. "How was he able to open a safe deposit box? You need an ID, right?"

"You do," she said. "He'd have had one."

"Who opened it for him?"

She glanced at the screen again, scrolling. A moment later, the color drained from her face. "I did." Swallowing hard, she blinked several times. "Oh. I think I need to sit down."

Agent Dye got up and pulled out the fourth chair.

Tess sank into it. "I'm so sorry. I don't know how this happened. I check IDs. In the past, I've turned people away for having fake ones." She propped her elbows on the table and covered her face, groaning.

"Tell us what you remember about him," Dye said.

She dropped her hands. "I'd need to see a picture."

Max glanced at Margot. "Hon, do you still have one?"

"Yeah." She took out her phone. "Somewhere." Expelling a long breath, she started scrolling.

"Ma'am, how far back do you keep surveillance footage?" Dye asked Tess.

"Ninety days."

"And when was the account opened?"

She glanced at her laptop screen. "June seventeenth, this year."

Margot stopped scrolling and looked at the manager in surprise.

"You're sure?" Max's tone turned sharp.

"Yes. It's right here." She gestured to the screen.

"That date mean something to you two?" Dye asked.

"It's the twins' birthday," Max replied.

Gallagher muttered a curse.

"Twins?" Dye arched an eyebrow in question.

"My daughters," Margot answered. "With Tad."

"Maybe this is a legacy for them." Max tipped his head, eyeing Margot. "We may not find anything at that location except the property itself. It could be why he left the key in your deposit box. He knows you rarely check it. That what you keep in there is an inheritance for the girls."

"But why the scavenger hunt? If it's a property for them, why wouldn't he just put the deed in my box? Why a betting ledger and a key to this safe deposit box?" She tipped her phone toward the metal container on the table.

Max scrunched his nose. She had a good point.

A moment later, she sat up straight. "I found one." Setting the phone on the table, she spun it around and pushed it toward Tess.

The woman picked it up, her brow scrunching. "He looks vaguely familiar, but nothing's jumping out at me." Face twisting, she looked at Agent Dye. "Sorry I can't be more help."

"It's all right. You're trying." Dye glanced across the table at Margot. "Keep that picture handy. We'll show it to the staff at your bank."

Margot nodded as she took her phone back.

Dye turned his phone around to speak to Agent Gallagher. "I'll call you later with updates about what we find at the other bank."

"Sounds good."

The two agents hung up, and Dye pocketed the phone.

"So, what now?" Max asked.

"Dr. Gaultier, with your permission, I'd like to take the contents of this box into evidence," Agent Dye said.

She nodded. "Of course."

The agent turned to Tess. "Ma'am, do you photocopy identification when people open accounts?"

"Yes."

"Could you make a copy of his ID for me?"

"Of course." She pushed her chair back. "Give me just a minute." Whirling on her heel, she hurried out of the room.

Dye reached into an interior pocket of his coat and produced several evidence bags. "Dr. Gaultier, may I have the journal and the jewelry pieces that were tampered with?"

Margot opened her purse and retrieved the items. Dye bagged them up, writing on the front with a sharpie.

Tess returned. "Here you go." She held out a sheet of paper to Agent Dye.

Max leaned forward, reading the address listed. It was the same address as the pin he'd dropped just minutes ago.

"Thank you, ma'am." Dye gave her a polite smile. "We're ready to put the box back now."

"Certainly." She picked it up and headed for the door.

Dye scooped up the evidence bags and followed her from the room.

Margot gave Max a quick look, then trailed behind the agent. Max picked up her purse and followed at a slower pace.

His mind whirled with possibilities of what they'd find at the property in Cass County. Everything from dead bodies to a stash of electronics Tad hadn't sold scrolled through his mind. Whatever it was, it had to shed some light on why Tad was in North Dakota.

He hoped.

Eighteen

Feeling decidedly zombie-like, Margot stumbled into their hotel room several hours later. They'd opted for one with two queens this time. It was playing with fire, but the specter of why they were here and what they were doing loomed over them and helped keep her in her own bed. That and the fact they'd yet to talk about that kiss.

Spying the perfectly made-up bed, she made a beeline for it, flopping onto her belly.

"Ugh. My brain is fried."

Once they left Ranchero Bank, Dye drove them to Westwood, where they spoke to the bank staff—none of whom copped to giving Tad access to her deposit box—and cleaned out what was left of her jewelry. She removed the coins, too, not trusting the staff.

From there, they visited Karl, the jeweler, again. He identified three more pieces that had stones replaced.

Anger burned in her belly at the thought. Even though she'd never wanted the items from her parents, it didn't mean she wasn't upset that Tad had stolen from her.

The bed dipped as Max sat down. His hand landed on her back and rubbed slow circles on her spine.

"You know what we need to do now, right?"

She turned her head to look at him. "What?"

"Call Asher."

Sighing, she rolled and sat up. "Let's get it over with. I want to open a new deposit box before you make me ride all the way over to Cass County."

Surprise flashed in his silvery blue eyes. "How did—?"

Margot rolled her eyes, a smile quirking one side of her mouth. "I know how you guys operate. You'll feed Asher all this information, and while he does a records search and maps the location, we'll drive over. By the time we get there, he'll have an entire history on the property, down to what color wallpaper was in the kitchen in 1952."

Max laughed. "Maybe not quite that detailed."

She waved a hand. "Close enough."

Still chuckling, he took out his phone and called Asher on FaceTime.

"Hey, guys. How's Texas?" Asher's smiling face appeared.

"Warmer than North Dakota," Margot said.

"And fruitful," Max said.

"Oh?" Asher arched an eyebrow. "Do tell."

Max chuckled. "We found the spare to that safe deposit box key I told you about. It was inside Margot's safe deposit box."

"What? Did you figure out what bank?"

"Yes. He left the key chain on it with the bank's logo. And we got into the deposit box. It contained a map with a property circled."

"Okay, hang on. Let me find some paper." Asher rose from his seat on the couch.

"I dropped a pin on it. Do you want me to just text it to you?"

"Sure." Dropping down to the plush gray cushions, Asher ran a hand through his hair. "Did you find anything else?"

"He replaced a bunch of the stones in Margot's jewelry with fakes, took two coins, and left behind a betting ledger. I think it's for horse racing."

"Damn. Do you have the journal?"

"No. The FBI does." A smile curved Max's mouth. "But I took pictures."

Asher grinned. "Perfect. Email them to me, and I'll see what I can get from them. So, you gave the feds all this information before me? I'm hurt." He pouted and laid a hand over his heart.

Margot laughed. "You're such a drama queen. We didn't want to ruin any evidence since Tad was murdered."

Asher sobered slightly. "I get it. Hopefully, with all of us working on this, we can solve it quickly. What's your next move?"

"We're going to check out that property. It's a few hours east of here."

"Don't go in. Not without the cops or unless it's life and death."

"We don't plan to." Max glanced at Margot, who shook her head. "I imagine Agent Gallagher will show up with a warrant in a day or so."

"No doubt. All right. I'll start researching the property as soon as we hang up."

"Great. Thanks, Asher." Max's thumb hovered over the disconnect button.

"Anytime. And if you need help, I'm a short plane ride away."

"How's Oregon treating you, anyway?" Max asked.

After the craziness that erupted there with Edie's sister, Esther, a couple of months ago, Asher had come home, packed up his house, and moved up there to be with her. Max was happy for him. Asher deserved the same happiness the rest of them had found.

He glanced at Margot from the corner of his eye. They still needed to have that chat about the kiss they shared. It had been... intense.

Amazing.

Life-changing.

Scary.

The intensity of it had blindsided him and was a huge factor in why he hadn't broached the subject. They'd been friends so long it was weird to think of her that way, but that kiss left little doubt there was more between them than friendship.

What he needed to do, though, was pull on his big boy pants and straight up ask her if she truly wanted a relationship with him.

"It's not bad. We're enjoying evenings by the fire. And the chilly, gray beach days are growing on me."

"Did you guys find a house yet?" Margot asked.

Asher's computers needed a dedicated space and were currently taking up the guest room at Esther's. They wanted a bigger place, so they had room for visitors.

"We did. It's out in the country, but we'll have plenty of room."

"That's great." A corner of Max's mouth tilted upward. "We'll have to come visit once you get settled in."

Asher chuckled. "Not all at once, please. We don't have that much room."

Margot gave a soft laugh. "You'd need Brooke's lodge to house all of us."

"That's no lie." Grinning, Asher shook his head. "All right. I'm going to go dig into your mystery property now. Send me those pictures and let me know if you uncover anything else."

"Will do," Max said. "Thanks, man."

"Yep." Asher waved. "See ya."

"Bye." Max tapped the disconnect button. He turned to Margot. "That's one task taken care of."

She smiled and leaned into him, wrapping her hands around his bicep and resting her chin on his shoulder. "Yeah. Sorry if I was a bit grumpy earlier. I'm mad."

He kissed her temple. "I know." It was on the tip of his tongue to suggest they do something to make her ungrumpy.

A slight increase in pressure behind his fly had him shifting. He leaned away from her, then stood. "Come on. Let's go check the next thing off our list."

Nineteen

A shiver crawled up Margot's spine.

This place was eerie.

She stared out the car window at the farmhouse they'd rolled up to. Backlit by the setting winter sun, the shadows only intensified the grime coating the once-white clapboard siding. Leafless vines crawled up the latticework around the base of the porch on the left side. It twined over the railing to climb the square posts holding up the porch roof and speared the tongue-and-groove ceiling, disappearing beneath the wood.

Behind the overgrown beautyberry shrubs, boards covered several broken panes in the front windows, giving the front of the house a patchwork look, though much less friendly and comforting than a quilt. A rusted, gray pickup sat in the gravel drive beside the house. It listed to the right, the rear tire flat.

"Well, I think it's safe to say no one's home." Max peered through the windshield. He cut the engine. "Let's take a look around."

The overhead light came on as he opened his door. Margot tugged on her doorhandle and got out.

Strands of her hair whipped over her eyes, and she snagged them with a finger, tucking the lock behind an ear. At least the breeze here was warmer. She'd packed her heavy parka away and donned a thick sweater. Texas was much more favorable than North Dakota for her tropical blood.

But a chill still crept through her.

Folding her arms over her chest, she followed Max up the driveway. They walked along the house, peering through grimy windows. The time of day made it difficult to see inside. Vague shapes filled the room. Margot squinted, making out a couch and a small table, but little else.

"I wish we could go inside." She cupped her hands around her eyes, leaning forward until less than an inch separated her skin from the window.

"Me too. But we don't need to give Gallagher even more reason to be suspicious. Your alibi for Tad's death is strong, but we all know killers can be hired."

Margot frowned and dropped her hands. When she turned, he had his phone out. The low ring of a call going through filled the air as he put it on speaker. "Who are you calling?" she asked.

"Asher."

The ringing stopped.

"Hello?" Asher's deep voice joined the rush of the wind.

"Hey, we're at the address I sent you. Did you find out anything about this place?" Max glanced up at the house. Their shoes crunched on the gravel drive as they wandered away from it and toward the outbuildings.

"I did. Property records show a Dale and Marie Conroy on the deed. I ran a search on them. Marie died about five years ago, but Dale's still alive. His driver's license shows that address."

"Really?" Max gave the house a skeptical look. "This place is pretty rundown. I can't imagine anyone living here."

"It's possible he moved out and didn't update his license. It's a couple of years old."

"They have any kids?" Margot asked.

"A son. He lives in St. Louis. So, I guess it's possible he's living up there."

"Okay," Max said. "We'll poke around here a little more. See if there's anything to point us to why Tad found this place important enough to put a map to it in a safe deposit box."

"Sounds good. If you need anything, call."

"You know it. Thanks, Asher."

"Yep. Talk to you soon."

"Bye." Max hung up.

Margot huffed. "This is bizarre. Who the heck is Dale Conroy? And how did Tad know him?"

"I don't know." Max put a hand on her back. "Come on. Let's check out the barn and shed."

Golden prairie grass whispered against their pant legs as they crossed the yard. She was glad it was winter. Most rattlesnakes would be holed up somewhere by now. They could come out on warmer days like today, but she'd expect to see them on rocks and not hiding in the tall grass where the sun couldn't reach them.

"I feel like if I imitated the Big Bad Wolf, I could huff and puff and blow this barn down," Max remarked as they approached the dilapidated structure.

Margot agreed. The building had definitely seen better days. Barely any red paint remained on the weathered wood siding—what was left of it. In several places, she could see through the barn all the way to the other side, and part of the roof had caved in toward the back. The rest looked ready to go. Even if they'd wanted to go inside, she wouldn't.

Stiff weed stems cracked under their feet as they moved closer. Like near the porch, beautyberry bushes grew wild, towering overhead. Margot studied the ones along the side of the barn. She couldn't help but wonder if they were holding the wall up.

They got as close as they dared, peeking through the gaps in the siding to see inside.

"We should have brought a flashlight." Margot squinted into the dim interior. Only the hulking skeletons of old machinery were visible in the waning light.

"Too conspicuous. Besides, I wasn't sure we'd even get this close." He glanced down, watching his footing as he found a path through the heavy brush toward an open door. "I'm not sure if it's a good thing or not that this place is abandoned." He stepped up to the door.

"Max!" Margot hissed. "Don't go in there."

"I'm not. Just trying to get a better look."

She huffed a breath through her nostrils, praying there was no sudden gust of wind while he stood so close.

Turning, she walked along the exterior; looking for what, she didn't know. Nothing seemed out of place. There wasn't anything she wouldn't expect to see at an abandoned country property. It was all falling down buildings and worn-out equipment. And weeds. Lots and lots of weeds.

The crunch of vegetation behind her told her Max had abandoned his desire to look in the barn and was catching up. Together, they headed for the shed.

It was in better shape. Probably because it looked like it was close to a hundred years newer. If she had to guess from the weathering on the steel siding and the dirty double-paned aluminum-framed windows, she'd say the shed was a decade or so old.

"That's weird."

"What is?" Margot glanced up. Max's gaze was fixed at a point beyond the shed.

"Nothing, really. It's just—" He paused and cocked his

head. "The grass is darker." Gaze still fixed on that point, he walked away.

"Max?" She stared after him for a moment, bewildered, then followed.

"Look at the vegetation. All around us, it's nothing but golden prairie grass. But back here..." His words trailed off as he stopped, staring at the ground.

Margot reached his side.

"Look." He extended a hand. "It's different. Greener."

Glancing down, her frown intensified. He was right. The prairie grass had gone dormant all around them.

Except here. There was still green in it.

"That's strange. Maybe there was something sitting here. A pile of fertilizer or something." She walked forward several feet, following the greener grass. Lifting a foot, she waved it through the vegetation.

A glint of something pale caught her eye. The sun was rapidly falling behind the trees, and in the thick vegetation, it was difficult to see what hid in its depths.

Margot pulled out her phone and turned on the flashlight, doubting anyone would see. She hadn't seen or heard a car in twenty minutes.

Her breath stalled in her lungs as the light illuminated the ground. A strangled shriek of surprise worked its way free, but her feet refused to move. So did her eyes. They were stuck on the sight before her.

"Margot?"

Max's voice removed the lock on her muscles. She stumbled back, inhaling a gulp of air. Extending a finger on the hand holding her phone, she pointed at the ground.

"It's—" Stopping, she clenched her teeth, the words sticking in her throat.

Swallowing hard, she tried again. "It's—look."

He frowned down at her for a moment before his gaze swung in the direction of her light.

She knew the moment he saw what she did. His eyes went wide and some of the color leached from his face.

Shining in the light from her phone, the hollowed eyes of a human skull stared back at them.

Max ran a hand down his face. "Fuck."

TWENTY

Headlights cut through the night, adding to the already illuminated scene at the farm. Max glanced toward the road to see a dark sedan come up the driveway. He assumed it was Agent Dye.

Once the shock of finding human remains wore off, he'd called the man, then the local police. The county sheriffs had been here for a couple of hours, roping things off and separating him from Margot so they could ask them questions.

She leaned against a cruiser twenty yards away, huddled into herself.

A wave of emotion washed over him, making his heart ache. He clenched his teeth. All he wanted to do was go to her and hold her.

The sedan rolled to a stop behind the cruiser. A moment later, the engine cut and the driver got out.

Agent Dye paused near the hood of his car, assessing the scene.

Max studied the agent.

He was young. Barely thirty, from the look of him. But intelligent. When they'd dealt with him earlier at the banks and at the jeweler's, he asked great questions and quickly made connections between bits of information.

Dye's gaze landed on Max.

The agent's expression held no anger. Just a curiousness. Max wasn't sure whether that was a good thing or not. On the one hand, it could be useful. It could make the man tenacious and determined to get justice. But it could put the Brigade's investigation in jeopardy. Most of what they did was aboveboard, but there was a certain bit of gray area in which they operated. Agent Dye's tenacity could force them out of things entirely. As much as Max wanted to be part of finding out what happened to Tad, he didn't want to go to jail for obstruction, nor did he want to put Asher and the others in that position, either.

Dye's attention shifted to the sergeant approaching. The two men spoke for a moment, then Dye followed him to the area behind the shed.

Max crossed his arms, continuing to study him.

The agent pulled a penlight from his coat and aimed it at the ground. Max watched him crouch, turn to speak to the crime scene technician nearby, then rise and put his light away. When he turned away, he headed toward Max, his strides determined.

Dye reached him, pausing several feet away. His light blue eyes studied Max.

Having perfected the art of nonchalance before this man was out of grade school, Max kept his arms crossed and stared right back.

Finally, Dye spoke. "What made you think it was a good idea to come out here?"

"Did you really expect us not to?"

A corner of the agent's mouth twitched. "All right. Did you touch anything?"

"No. We walked around the house, then the barn and the

shed. I noticed the greener prairie grass, and when we shined a light on it, we saw the skull. I called you, then the local police."

"Do you know who it is?"

Max arched an eyebrow. "Why would I?"

Dye shrugged one shoulder. "You know a lot of other things about this investigation. Agent Gallagher mentioned he agreed to work with you and your 'team.'" He made air quotes.

Annoyance tickled Max's mind. "Perhaps you should drop the 'I'm the agent' attitude, then. Margot and I aren't the bad guys."

With a quick puff of air through his nostrils, Dye stuffed his hands in his pockets and glanced away briefly. "What has your team learned about the victim?"

"Nothing."

Dye threw up his hands. "Come on, man. Why are you being difficult? We worked together all afternoon without a problem."

It was Max's turn to look away. "Sorry. I don't much like being questioned as though I murdered someone." He tipped his head toward the deputies milling about the property. "They separated us as soon as they got here, then grilled us about who we were, who that is"—he nodded toward the remains—"and why we were here. Over and over again."

"That's standard protocol."

"Doesn't mean I like it. But to answer your question, I don't know who the victim is. It's possible it's the property owner, Dale Conroy, though."

Something akin to admiration crossed Dye's face. "You know who owns this place already?"

"It was a simple records search. It's owned by Dale and Marie Conroy. Marie's dead. Has been for five years. Her husband has an active driver's license that comes back to this address. He's not here, and it looks like no one has been for a while. That could be him."

"There's more than a few months of neglect here, though." Dye circled a finger in the air. "Forensics said whoever that is has been dead less than a year. Just in their preliminary examination, they found small amounts of tissue on the bones."

Max shrugged. "Like I said, it's just a theory. But maybe inside the house there will be something that tells us more."

"Maybe. What else do you know?"

"That's it."

"Nothing that connects the Conroys to Dr. Gaultier? Not her." He nodded toward Margot. "Her ex."

"No. Not so far."

Dye rolled his lips in, pressing them together. "All right. Hang out here for a bit. I want to talk to the sergeant again. See where we are on a warrant to search the place."

"They have a son. In St. Louis. Maybe see if Mr. Conroy's there and get permission to search the house? It'd be quicker than a warrant."

Amusement lit Dye's face. "You got a name and number for the son?"

"I can get it."

"How about you do that while I go talk to the sergeant?"

"Can I stand with Margot now?"

The agent's gaze turned to her. She was still huddled at the back of the cruiser, watching the forensic team comb the grass for evidence.

"Sure. Just stay visible."

"Not a problem." Max dropped his arms and started toward Margot.

In moments, he reached her. "Hey."

She jumped, letting out a soft yelp. "Hey. Sorry. I wasn't paying attention."

He touched her arm. "I can tell. You all right?"

Inhaling a deep breath through her nose, she nodded. "Yeah. What are you doing over here? The police wanted us to stay separate."

"Dye's here." He nodded toward the agent.

Margot turned.

"We had a little chat. I need to call Asher again." He pulled his phone out. Taking a quick glance around to make sure no one was eavesdropping, he dialed and put the call on speaker so Margot could hear.

"Hey. All done?" Asher asked.

"Not quite. Margot and I found some skeletal remains."

Only a slight crackle on the line for several beats told Max the call was still active.

"Come again? Hell," Asher muttered. "Are you serious?"

"I wish I wasn't. Anyway, the cops and Agent Dye are here. Can you get me a name and phone number for Dale Conroy's son?"

"Sure. Give me a sec."

Soft noises came over the line as Asher moved around. They heard the low murmur of Esther's voice, then Asher's reply that everything was fine. A moment later, typing sounded.

"Okay. Let's see what we've got here." Another pause came over the line, then, "The son's name is Edward. I'll text you the number and address. Do you have any idea who the body is? Is it the owner, Dale?"

"We don't know. Forensics said whoever it is has been dead less than a year. My guess is sometime over the summer. He or she's covered in prairie grass, which is much greener than anywhere else."

"Damn. Okay. Keep me posted, yeah? I'll help however I can. I just sent that info."

A banner appeared at the top of the screen with a text from Asher.

"It came through. Can you run a search for a connection between the Conroys and Tad?"

"Already am, but I'll double down on it."

"Great. Thanks, Asher." Max glanced around.

"Yep."

Dye and the sergeant approached.

"Gotta go. Bye."

"Later."

Max hung up. He cast a quick look at Margot, whose expression looked rather pinched. Reaching out, he took her hand briefly and squeezed it reassuringly. Tad's death was growing more complicated by the second.

"You get that info?" Dye asked.

"Yep." Max switched to his texts and opened the one from Asher. "You got a pen and paper?"

Dye pulled a notebook from his pocket. "Fire away."

Max read off the information.

The agent's mouth quirked upward as he finished writing. He shook his head, clicking his pen. "Whoever was on the end of that call, you need to persuade them to come work for the bureau."

Max scoffed. "Even if I was so inclined, he never would." Asher had been there and done that and had zero desire to ever do it again.

"He could do a lot of good on this side of the law."

He held Dye's gaze, silently telegraphing it was time to change the subject. "He does a lot of good right where he is." Max tipped a finger at the notebook in the agent's hand. "How about you call that number and find out if Dale Conroy is in St. Louis?"

The sergeant, who'd been standing there listening, arched an eyebrow at Max's tone, but wisely stayed out of it.

Dye's expression soured. He stared at Max for several seconds, then seemed to decide it wasn't worth it to argue. Shaking his head, he took out his phone and dialed.

Max could hear the quiet buzz of the line ringing. It cut off after four rings, and he heard the low murmur of a man's voice.

"Hello. I'm sorry to bother you. I'm trying to reach Dale Conroy." Dye's voice took on a friendly tone, the serious agent evaporating.

Straining to hear, Max leaned closer, but all he could hear was a muffled male voice.

"Oh, I see. I'm sorry to hear that. Mr. Conroy, my name is Agent Jeremiah Dye. I'm with the FBI. We have reason to believe your parents' farm is connected to a case we're working on. Now, I know your mother passed away several years ago, correct?"

Max heard the man utter a single syllable. It sounded like he said yes.

"And you said you haven't had any contact with your dad since then. He's not here, and we're concerned about his well-being. The property is extremely rundown. Would you give us permission to conduct a welfare check and go inside the house and other buildings on the property?"

Max fought the urge to tap his foot while he waited on Dye to finish his conversation. The agent could have had the courtesy to put the call on speaker.

"Thank you. Would you like me to let you know if we find him?"

Dye's eyebrows shot up, and he shook his head. "All right. I guess if you hear from me again, you'll know. Thank you for your time. Have a nice evening." He hung up.

"Well?" Max arched a brow.

"Mr. Conroy and his father are not on good terms. He told me they haven't spoken since his mother died and that the only way he wants me to call him back is if it's to tell him the old man's dead."

Max let out a low whistle.

"Damn," the sergeant said. "That's cold."

"I'm sure he has his reasons. In any case, he gave us permission to conduct a welfare check. I'll keep the warrant coming, but this might at least give us a place to start. Let's go round up a few of your deputies. No pictures, though. Not unless we find another body. Anything else will have to wait until my warrant comes through."

"Understood. I'll go grab a few men and meet you at the back door."

"Thank you."

With a nod, the sergeant sauntered away.

Dye turned to Max. "I'm sorry. I can't invite you inside until we have the warrant, and the forensics team has a chance to conduct their investigation."

"I figured. All I ask is that you tell us if you see anything suspicious."

"I can do that." Dye backed away. "Hang here. I'll be back." Turning, he strode toward the house.

Max blew out a breath and scrubbed his hands over his face and then through his hair. "This is nuts."

A mirthless laugh escaped Margot's lips. "Tell me about it. I thought I knew Tad. None of this—including the way he left me—feels like anything he would do."

"Maybe whoever that is out there"—he nodded toward the shed—"will give us a clue as to why he did what he did." Extending an arm, he tugged her closer to envelop her in a hug.

"I hope so," she murmured against his chest, her head snuggled under his chin. "I'm tired of all the drama."

"Me too." He placed a soft kiss on top of her head. Deep down, he yearned to be back in Costa Rica, this woman tucked into his side while they watched Em and Lily play in the sunshine. He just wanted all this to be a distant memory.

Thirty minutes passed while they waited on the police to coordinate with each other and walk through the house. When they emerged from behind the building, the scowl on Agent Dye's face put Max's senses on alert.

He nudged Margot, who now rested next to him against the cruiser. "They found something."

"What?"

He didn't need to look at her to hear the frown in her voice.

"How do you know?"

"Dye's face. That look says it all." He took her hand. "Come on."

They met the agent in a pool of light under the saltpeter lights the crime scene unit set up.

"Is it another body?" Max asked.

"No." Dye ran a hand through his short hair. "There's no sign of Dale Conroy. But there was a bag of money in plain view on the kitchen table."

Max blinked several times before his brain processed that. "A bag of money? Like banded bills?"

"Yeah. Whoever that is"—he pointed to where forensics still worked by the shed—"they weren't killed for the cash."

TWENTY-ONE

Margot shifted, smothering a yawn as she tried valiantly to stay awake. She never should have sat down. But they'd been here for hours now and she'd been freezing. Once the sun finally eclipsed the horizon, the temperature had dropped dramatically. When Agent Dye told her she was welcome to have a seat in the car, she'd jumped at the chance to bask in the heater's warmth.

But now she was toasty, and it had made her sleepy.

Yawning again, she sat up and blinked as she peered through the windshield. Half an hour or so ago, Agent Dye had walked up and crooked a finger at Max. He'd asked Margot if she wanted to come, too, but she'd already been rapidly fading and had opted to stay in the car. Max would fill her in on anything she needed to know.

Now, the two men were walking around the side of the house, and Dye had a tan duffel in his gloved hand.

She hit the button to turn off the car and got out. The chilly breeze immediately penetrated her sweater. For a moment, she debated digging her parka out of the back, but it was stuffed—and she meant *stuffed*—into her suitcase, and she didn't feel like making a mess of the cargo area.

Hugging herself, she rounded the hood and waited for them to reach her.

"Did you get warmed up?" Max stopped an arm's length away and ran a soft hand down her arm.

"Yes." She looked at Dye. "Is that the money?"

"It is."

Her gaze bounced between the men. She didn't like the pinch to Max's expression. "What else did you find? And don't even think about telling me nothing. I can see by the look on your face there's more."

Dye answered, not giving Max a chance. "Another map."

Margot sighed. Closing her eyes, she lifted one hand and pressed her fingers to her forehead.

"It has handwriting on it."

Max's words brought her head up.

"Can you take a look at it? Tell us if it's Tad's?" Dye asked.

She dropped her arms. "Sure."

Walking past her, Dye set the duffel on the hood of the car, then opened his coat to remove an evidence bag. From another pocket, he produced a pair of gloves. "Put these on, please."

Margot took the purple gloves and put them on while he pulled the map from the bag and carefully unfolded it.

He pointed to the margin. "There."

Tipping her head, she leaned in, trying to get a better look. Shadows crisscrossed the surface over here away from the bright lights.

"Hang on." Dye reached into yet another pocket and produced a small penlight.

With the surface illuminated, it only took her a moment to know it was indeed Tad's handwriting. "That's his. What does that mean, though?" Scrawled at the edge of the map in black ink was a single word: Chase. Another circle, like on the first map, highlighted an area of interest.

"It's a bank," Max said. "We looked at what's inside that circle. There's a Chase Bank location."

"And it was robbed thirteen months ago," Dye added.

Margot's knees wobbled. "What?" She turned round eyes on Max.

His gaze was steady but wary. "Did Tad spend any time in Shreveport?"

"Not that I know of. Is that where the bank is?"

He nodded.

"I really don't think so. I mean, he came home really late many nights, but not drove to Shreveport and back late."

"What about work trips?" Dye asked.

"No. We didn't take too many of those. Conferences, but those were with other people from the hospital and nowhere near Shreveport."

"Okay. If you can give me places and some names of people he went with, that would be great."

Margot rolled her lips in and nodded once. "I'll have to think on it a bit. A lot's happened since then." Not to mention, her brain wasn't fully functional right now. Shock, fatigue, and the cold had stolen her processing power.

"Of course. As soon as you can."

Inhaling a deep breath, she stared over his shoulder for a moment. "Is that all you found? Anything connecting Tad to this place?"

"No. That's still a mystery, unfortunately."

Margot shared a look with Max. They'd be making another phone call to Asher tonight.

"Do you mind if we head out now?" Max asked Dye. "It's been a long day, and we'd like to get some rest."

"Of course. Where are you staying?" Dye refolded the map.

"Not sure yet. We drove straight here. I'll text you when we settle somewhere."

"Sounds good." Stuffing the map into the evidence bag, he sealed it up again. "Keep me apprised of anything you uncover."

Smile tight, Max nodded. "We'll touch base tomorrow. Have a good night."

Dye's mouth tipped in a sardonic smile. "Oh, it'll be a blast."

Twenty-Two

A soft trill penetrated Max's consciousness. Blinking slowly, he lifted his head, still half-asleep, and realized the noise was coming from his phone on the nightstand. A quick glance at the clock almost had him ignoring it. It wasn't Asher or any of his friends back home calling. He didn't need to look to know that.

But considering the events of the last several days, it could be important.

Scooping up the phone, he answered. "Hello?"

"You up?"

It was Agent Dye.

"No. It's six-thirty. Have you even slept?"

"I got a couple hours. I'm downstairs. Get yourselves down here." He hung up.

Max stared at the now silent rectangle. What the hell was that all about?

Easing the covers back, he got up. Quickly donning a pair of jeans and snagging his key card from the dresser, he left his room and knocked on Margot's door.

When she didn't answer after thirty seconds, he knocked

again, louder. He wouldn't doubt that she was dead to the world. They'd both been exhausted when they checked in last night, and she'd been so very weary, emotionally. He'd almost offered to hold her all night, but knew that could have easily turned into more. And he didn't want her to think that had been his goal all along. When they finally gave in to their desire, he didn't want there to be any question about his intentions—or hers.

A soft thump sounded on the other side of the door, then a light came on, shining through the crack at his feet.

The security chain rattled, then he came face-to-face with a sleepy Margot. His stomach clenched. She looked so soft and alluring straight from bed. He wanted to wrap his arms around her and take her right back from where she'd come.

Instead, he cleared his throat and passed on Dye's message. "Agent Dye just called. He's downstairs and wants to meet with us."

She brushed her hair back from her face. "Now?"

"I know, but it must be important."

"Yeah. All right. Give me a few minutes to get dressed."

He stepped back. "Meet out here in five?"

She nodded and closed the door.

Reversing direction, Max went back to his room and threw on some clothes, then brushed his teeth. He skipped shaving, and soon had his feet stuffed into his shoes. Key card in hand, he was out the door.

Carpet muffled his footsteps in the empty hallway as he moved to wait outside Margot's room. Leaning against the wall, he crossed his arms. A yawn overtook him, and he raised a hand to cover it.

Normally, he was an early riser, preferring to be up before the sun and get a workout in. But it had been nearly impossible to fall asleep last night. Despite his exhaustion, his mind had simply refused to shut off. All the facts about the case kept swirling through his mind. Nothing made any more sense now than it did when he went to bed.

Margot's door opened, and she stepped out. He missed the sleepy Margot, but this fresh-faced, rushed one was just as beautiful.

"Ready?" He pushed off the wall.

"Yep. Let's go find out what's so damn important it couldn't wait until a normal hour."

Heading down the hall, they took the elevator to the ground floor. When the doors opened, he spotted Dye in the lobby. He stood with another man Max didn't recognize.

Dye glanced up at the sound of the elevator. Nudging the man next to him, they started forward.

"Thanks for coming down. Sorry it's so early, but things took a twist." Dye glanced at his companion. "This is U.S. Marshal Kyle Marchand."

"U.S. Marshals?" Max's eyebrows dipped into a low vee. Why were they involved now? The FBI handled bank robberies.

A businessman, holding a steaming cup of coffee, slipped around them, pulling a rolling suitcase.

"Let's go find a seat out of the way, shall we?" Marchand gestured to a grouping of chairs on the far side of the lobby. "Then I'll explain why I'm here."

Max sent a quick glance at Margot. She looked as perplexed as he was.

The four of them crossed the lobby and sat down on the deep purple, faux-leather seats.

"As Agent Dye said, I'm sorry to haul you out of bed, but this is potentially time-sensitive."

"What is?" Margot leaned forward. "I don't understand."

"Your husband confided in one of my counterparts at the FBI—an undercover agent—about eighteen months ago. He had evidence of a betting ring that had turned violent."

The blood drained from Margot's face. Max could only imagine what was going through her mind. How she felt.

He didn't have to wonder about how he felt, though. Anger boiled his blood. Why hadn't they known about this from the beginning? "Why are we just learning of this?" He aimed a glare at Dye, then shifted it to Marchand. "Did you not know about this? Why didn't Gallagher? They've had his name for weeks."

Marchand leaned forward and propped his elbows on his knees, pinning Max with a hard stare. "They didn't know because Tad Gaultier's identity was protected. Dr. Gaultier, your ex-husband entered WitSec."

Twenty-Three

Margot knew she looked like a fish, mouth gaping, closing, then gaping again, but she couldn't force any words past the air frozen in her throat.

Luckily, Max didn't seem to have that problem.

"Are you fucking serious?" His booming voice carried through the lobby. Pushing to his feet, he walked to the window. Margot's gaze followed him. She agreed with the sentiment.

He spun around to glare at Marshal Marchand. "Why would he go into WitSec and not take Margot and the kids? Wouldn't they still be in danger?"

Marchand glanced away for a brief moment, his expression souring. "At the time, no."

His wording removed the block from Margot's voice, and she turned to face him. "What do you mean, 'At the time'? Is there danger now?" Her heart thumped and did a quick flip in her chest.

The girls!

"We need to call Dean." She surged out of her chair and turned panicked eyes on Max, who already had his phone out.

Marchand patted the air. "Let's slow down. I agree, we need to put some protections in place, but may I explain first?"

A burst of anger pushed away some of the fright filling her chest. Spinning around, she pinned him with an icy glare. "That would be a wonderful idea, yes."

The marshal didn't waste time. "Your ex-husband borrowed money from a small criminal organization the FBI has been watching for some time. One of their undercover operatives embedded in the horse racing scene buddied up to him, got to know him a bit. The plan was to catch Tad making illegal bets and force his hand so he would testify against the group. But before that could happen, he defaulted on his payments again. And when I say again, I mean for probably the fourth or fifth time. The head of this organization, Devin Owens, decided he'd had enough and threatened to expose Tad to the hospital board." Marchand's gaze flicked to Max, who watched with his arms crossed, phone clutched in his hand so hard his knuckles were white.

"It freaked Tad out," Marchand continued. "He didn't know that Owens knew who he was. He'd given a fake name. Thomas Villanova."

Her jaw worked as she seethed. Was that the only reason Tad was scared? Because he'd lose his medical license? What about what could have happened to their family?

"Our operative cornered Tad shortly after that. By then, he had enough evidence to bring charges against your ex for fraud and illegal gambling. And he offered him an option: testify against Owens or face charges."

Max held up a finger. "One thing doesn't make sense. How did he end up in WitSec? Threatening to expose someone doesn't sound particularly violent."

"It's not. But the people Owens partnered with are."

Margot frowned, the fear creeping back in to spread dark tendrils through her body. What did that mean?

Marchand noticed the change in her demeanor and held up a hand. "I'm getting there, I promise. So, the FBI only had bits and pieces of evidence against Owens. They needed something bigger. Something that would put him away for many years and dismantle his criminal enterprise, or it would just spring back up under his minions. The operative convinced Tad to cooperate. They gave him enough cash to pay off some of his debts and get him back into the fold. It worked. He was back in and soon gained more of Owens's trust. Enough to make him offer Tad an opportunity to get completely square."

"The bank robbery." Max dropped his arms and walked closer, stopping beside Margot.

She shuffled her feet until her shoulder touched his arm, needing the physical touch to calm the riot of emotions bouncing around her head.

Marchand nodded. "Exactly. And this is where the violent partners come in. Owens had grand plans. He wanted to be like Benny Binion, an old-timey bookie and hotelier. But opening a fancy hotel takes seed money, and he was having trouble getting investors. No one wanted to take on a project like that from an unknown, who didn't have backing already. It was a catch twenty-two for Owens; he needed investors to get investors. So, his plan was to set up a shell corporation and funnel the robbery money through there. Make it look legit so he could persuade others to invest."

Marchand paused, eyeing another traveler who walked past. Standing, the marshal eased closer, and once the man was out of earshot, he continued. "Tad was the getaway driver."

"If the FBI knew all of this, why let them go ahead with the robbery?" Max aimed a questioning glare at Dye. "Why wouldn't the place be full of undercover agents, ready to take them down?"

Slowly, Dye rose from his seat, casting a quick glance at Marchand. "That was the plan. From what I understand. I only know what he knows." He pointed at the marshal. "It's not my case."

"There was a whole, elaborate op in the works. But Fred Berry, the head of the robbery gang, got antsy and jumped the gun."

"Okay, so they robbed the bank and took off with Tad at the wheel. How did he end up with you?" Max tipped a finger toward Marchand.

"Berry tried to kill him."

Margot covered her mouth, feeling tears well in her eyes.

Jesus. Why hadn't he come to her? Sure, she'd have been upset, but they could have done something to pay off his debts and get him help. She could have sold the jewelry her parents left her, or a couple of the coins. At least it would have kept him out of danger.

"Apparently, it was a snap decision and Berry's a bad shot," Dye said.

Marchand shifted, casting a quick glance around the lobby. "Tad said he was standing by the car, and when Berry pulled out the gun, he dove into the driver's seat and just took off. We found a bullet embedded in the bumper, but no other marks."

"Why didn't he come straight to his FBI contact?" Max asked.

"Fear of repercussions," Marchand answered. "Berry shot and killed the bank manager during the robbery. He was afraid he'd get charged with accessory to commit murder. He'd also lost confidence in the agency's ability to keep him safe after the robbery went so off the rails."

"Okay, so how did Tad end up with you and why was the money at the Conroy's farm? How do they figure into this?" Max crossed his arms again, a deep frown on his face.

"When Tad ran after the robbery, the money was in the car. He told us he spent months on the run, trying to stay one step ahead of Berry, but he was running low on funds and didn't want to use the robbery money. Hence the reason he finally turned himself in. One of his caveats to working with us again was withholding where he'd stashed the money. He said he wasn't giving it up until we could assure his safety and yours." Marchand nodded to Margot. "Even though he'd already left you, Dr. Gaultier, several months before, he didn't want any of the kickback, if he got caught, to fall on you. So, we put him in witness protection and put a detail on you and your daughters."

"I'm sorry, what?" Eyes narrow, she leaned in, not sure she'd heard him right. They'd been followed? She balled her fists, tamping down the anger that wanted to explode from her mouth in a loud and expletive-filled rant. If she'd been under suspicion of wrongdoing, she could accept being followed without her knowledge. But when it was her safety and her daughters' safety on the line, she should have been informed of the danger. She'd have been more vigilant and cognizant of her surroundings.

Max held up a hand. She looked at him and saw the raw anger simmering in his eyes. "Why wouldn't you take Margot and the girls too? Owens knew Tad's real name and what he did for a living. It wouldn't be hard to find out about his family, especially since Margot worked in the same hospital."

"We offered that to him, but he said he didn't think Owens would let Berry resort to that. Despite his criminal ways, Owens has scruples. He—"

Max sliced a hand through the air. "No. Wrong answer. You should never have bowed to Tad's wishes. Not with a violent criminal in the midst."

"He threatened to walk, Mr. Carson. The entire case

would have just—poof"—he raised a closed hand and popped it open—"disappeared without him."

"So, the lives of a woman and two children were inconsequential, is what you're saying?"

Marchand narrowed his eyes. A muscle ticked in his jaw. "No. But as I said, even with what we knew about Berry, we didn't think Dr. Gaultier or her children were in any real danger. But to be sure, we posted a protective detail." He turned his gaze to Margot. "Then you went and helped us out by leaving. At that point, we figured you and your daughters were relatively safe. Especially once we learned you'd surrounded yourself with several former members of the special forces."

Margot poked her tongue into her cheek and glanced through the front windows as she digested that. It still didn't sit right with her that they'd left her in the dark.

She returned her gaze to the marshal and cast a quick glance at Agent Dye, encompassing him with her next question. "Why do you think we need protection now? Tad's dead. The feds have the money. Why are my girls and I still in danger?"

"Because Berry doesn't know we have the money," Dye said.

Marchand's lips flattened. "I've been monitoring the FBI's investigation into the body found in North Dakota. That postcard you identified in your ex-husband's things set off alarm bells for me. I think Berry's been in Costa Rica and was trying to scare Tad into giving up the money. We're worried he'll escalate things."

Margot's eyes narrowed, confused. She glanced at Max to see the same confusion on his face.

"Why would he escalate things?" Margot asked. "He killed Tad."

Dye's expression tightened, and a pit formed in Margot's stomach.

Marchand inhaled a breath, then dropped a bomb.

"Tad's not dead."

TWENTY-FOUR

Max's eyebrows slammed down. He could feel his neck and face turning red as fury swelled. In contrast, all the blood drained from Margot's face, leaving her white as a sheet. Her nails dug into his bicep as she clutched his arm.

A moment later, she let go of him and stumbled to a chair, sitting down. Max moved behind her, laying his hands on her shoulders, not only to offer her comfort but to keep them occupied so he didn't do something dumb, like deck a federal agent.

He pierced Marchand with a fierce glare. "Why are we just now learning this? The FBI has had Tad's car for weeks. If Margot and the kids were in danger, why hasn't someone contacted her? We'd have been more vigilant and might have seen someone lurking." And he sure as hell never would have left the country to help Sam. Nor would he have left the twins behind on this trip. They'd have brought them along—with backup.

"We didn't have any evidence Berry was still in Costa Rica. Or that he'd ever been. He could have paid someone to mail that postcard."

Max hummed. "Didn't have any evi—" he stopped himself, pressing his lips together. Pulling in a breath through his nose, he tamped down the urge to throttle Marchand. He wouldn't get the answers to all his questions if the man was unconscious. "Where's Tad now?"

"Blissfully unaware of any of this."

In one smooth movement, Margot was out of her chair and only steps away from Marchand. "Why? If you knew he was alive, why did I go to Minot to identify his things? If you wanted to keep me out of this, why involve me in that?"

"That ball was in motion before I could say anything. Then, I didn't want to tip our hand, so I stayed out of it and let you come." He glanced away briefly. "I also wanted to see what information you could add."

Her brows dipped so low they nearly touched. Max saw her muscles tense and knew she was about to do what he'd been trying not to.

In two quick strides, he was around the chair and had her wrapped in his arms. "Easy, babe."

She pushed against his arms, but he held on tight. "Are you serious right now? This jackass put Emily and Lily in danger. Why aren't you helping me beat his face in?"

Max eyed the marshal over her shoulder, letting the man see the fury he kept banked. "Trust me, I want to. But we need him and the answers he has locked in his brain."

Marchand's spine stiffened. He met Margot's gaze. "For what it's worth, it wasn't personal, and if I'd believed you or your daughters were in any real danger, I would have made you aware."

Was he for real?

Max rolled his eyes and debated letting Margot go. The guy just didn't get it.

"I'm upset about that, yes," Margot said. "But right now, I want to break your nose because you used me! And you let me believe someone I once loved was dead! Someone who, despite his faults, still means something to me."

Her voice reached a pitch that carried through the lobby. Several people stopped and turned to look at them.

Marchand glanced around, a tight, polite smile on his face. He nodded to a couple of people.

"I know you want to know where he is," he said, turning back to them. "But I can't tell you that." He kept his voice low. "Not until we have Berry in custody."

Max ground his molars together. He wanted to press the man for more on Tad's whereabouts, but the set to his face told him it would be as pointless as a worn pencil. "If he's not the body the fisherman found, who is it?"

"We think it's Owens."

"You think?" Max's eyebrows went skyward. "Have you asked Tad? What does he say?"

Dye sent a derisive look at the marshal, surprising Max. Apparently, something didn't sit right with the agent.

"They haven't," Dye said.

Marchand cast an annoyed glance at his counterpart. "As I said, we want Dr. Gaultier to stay unaware of things for now, so no. We haven't asked him about who could be the man pulled from the lake."

"Of all the—" Margot started, but Marchand waved a hand.

"I'm not getting into that with you. Nor am I willing to clue your ex-husband in on what's happening at the moment. We need him to stay where he is. He's our only witness to any of this, and we need him alive. As I said, we think the deceased is Owens. The current working theory is that Berry got greedy. Perhaps Owens wouldn't let him go after Tad's family. With Owens out of the way, he's free to get the cash however he sees fit."

"He'd really kill a woman and two young children for

what, fifty grand? A hundred grand, if they split it fifty-fifty?" They'd found two hundred thousand dollars in the duffel bag at the farmhouse.

"Actually," Dye said, "it's probably a lot more than that. We were at the Conroy's property until all hours of the morning. My team found a literal barrel full of cash in the barn. It was over a million dollars. The day they robbed the bank, they'd just gotten a truck. Payday was the next day for one of the area's major employers."

Max tipped his head back and ran a hand over his face. This was turning into an insane mess. "How is Conroy connected? He hasn't been dead since the robbery, right?"

"No." Dye shook his head. "We're still not sure about that."

"I ran the name against Berry and Owens's known associates," Marchand added. "No one with that name is connected to either of them. That we know of." He turned to Margot. "Dr. Gaultier, are you sure you don't know the Conroys? Or that your ex-husband doesn't?"

"I have no idea who they are. As for whether Tad knows them, you'll have to ask him."

Something flashed in Marchand's gaze. Annoyance, perhaps. And a bit of anger at her flippant attitude.

Max bit back a mirthless grin. Good. The marshal deserved everything Margot dished out for keeping them in the dark like this.

"What are you doing about Margot and the girls' safety?" Max pinned the man with a hard stare. He wanted to make sure there was a backup layer in place. He had full confidence in his friends, but this was Emily and Lily's safety they were talking about. As far as he was concerned, there could never be enough eyes watching out for them.

"Two of my colleagues are boarding a plane to Costa Rica as we speak. They'll become Emily and Lily's shadows. I will escort you and Dr. Gaultier home. We've already cleared it with the Costa Rican authorities."

Crossing his arms, Max continued to give Marchand a hard look. Part of him wanted to tell the man to shove it where the sun didn't shine. But for Margot and the girls' safety, they all needed to cooperate. That didn't mean he'd let the marshal run roughshod over him, though. "Fine. But you and your colleagues will play a backseat to myself and our friends. No offense, but I don't know you. However, I do know my friends and what they're capable of. There's no one I trust more than them to keep Margot and the girls safe." He cast a quick look at Margot, hoping she didn't think he was speaking out of turn. The protection was for her, not him. But she didn't look upset. Not at him, anyway.

Still, he decided to ask her. "Is that all right with you, Margot?"

"Yes." She looked at Marchand. "You and the other marshals can watch from outside. My girls and I will stick close to Max and our friends."

The marshal's lips flattened, and the hard glare he aimed at Max said he wasn't pleased. "We'll discuss it when we get there."

Max bit back a snort. No, they wouldn't.

He let his arms fall back to his sides. "Do you have any other bombshells to drop, or can we go call our friends to fill them in?"

Marchand's face relaxed. "I'm all done. Except to say I've booked the three of us on a flight out of Dallas this afternoon. Once you call your friends, pack up and meet me back down here. We need to get on the road."

With a nod, Max motioned for Margot to stand. "Text me the info on your colleagues. I'll forward it to my friends, so they know who to look for. Dye has my number."

He held out a hand to Margot. "Shall we?"

Blue eyes flinty, she aimed an icy glare at the marshal. "Yes. Get me out of here before I poke his eyes out."

Without another word—mostly because he wanted to do the same thing and was holding on to his temper by a thread—he ushered her away.

TWENTY-FIVE

A numbness had settled over Margot's mind on the ride up from the lobby, replacing the anger.

She sank onto the bed in Max's room and stared at the wall. It was like she was above everything, watching the drama unfold around her; not really part of it.

But she knew she was. This really was her life.

Tad was alive.

A killer wanted to change that.

He might want to kill her and her daughters too.

Max's face filled her field of vision, and his warm hands covered her icy ones.

"Hey. Are you all right?"

She sucked in a sharp breath through her nose. Glancing away, she blinked several times, ridding herself of the sudden moisture that gathered in her eyes. Was she?

"I don't know," she finally whispered.

The bed dipped as Max sat beside her. He wrapped an arm around her shoulders and kissed her temple. "I'm sorry, Margot."

The simple, heartfelt kindness in his voice was enough to make the tears return to her eyes.

That was enough to make her angry again, but for a different reason. She'd cried all she wanted to over Tad. And she was done letting him have a say in her life.

Swiping at her face, she shrugged out of Max's hold and stood. "Call Dean. Make sure my babies are safe."

He stared up at her for a long moment, his blue eyes studying hers, concern shining from their depths. She willed him to drop it. She wasn't in the mood to talk about her feelings.

Thankfully, he seemed to sense that, because a moment later, he stood and nodded. Taking his phone from his pocket, he dialed Dean's number, putting the call on speaker.

The line rang several times, echoing through the hotel room. Margot thought it would roll to voicemail, but a sleepy-sounding Dean finally answered.

"'Lo?" His gravely voice told her he'd been asleep.

"Hey. So, there have been some developments," Max began.

Dean's yawn ended on a disbelieving huff. "More than what you and Asher told us about last night?"

"Yeah. Tad's alive."

Dead silence came over the line. Then, "Shit. Did he show up?"

"No. A U.S. Marshal did. Tad's in WitSec. It's complicated, but the gist of it is there's a psychotic and greedy bank robber looking for him, who will stop at nothing to get his money. There are two marshals heading down there to keep an eye on the twins. Another is escorting Margot and me home this afternoon."

"Well, crap. All right. I'll call the others, and we'll batten down security around here. Do you have flight details? One of us can come get you."

"Not yet, but I'll make sure to get it. Marchand—the marshal we met with—sent me dossiers on the two marshals coming to you." He clicked into his text messages.

Margot frowned, wondering when that happened. Must have been on the elevator ride up. As the anger had faded to numbness, she'd tuned most everything out.

"I'll try to get you an image of the guy we're looking for too. You could put Asher on that. I'm not sure how forthcoming this marshal will be with information. The guy's name is Fred Berry. He partnered with a man named Devin Owens. The latter is a bookie in the Dallas area who mostly ran bets on horse racing. Not sure how he knows Berry, but they robbed a Chase bank in Shreveport, Louisiana."

Dean yawned again. "Okay. I'll call him."

"Are the girls doing all right?" Margot asked. They'd seemed fine when she spoke to Annabeth yesterday, but now she was doubly worried about being away from them.

"They're fine. Keeping us hopping. Emily decided she wanted to surf yesterday. She saw my board and demanded to try it. So, I took her out, and we rode some small waves in on our bellies. She loved it. I even got Lily to try it."

Margot's eyebrows shot up. Her youngest twin was not adventurous at all. She much preferred watching to doing. "Really? Did she like it?"

"She did. I was surprised too."

"We'll have to have Edie set them up with some body-boards. They're getting to be pretty good swimmers, so I think they'll do all right with that." Max glanced at her.

Of all the things she thought her daughters would do at such a young age, surfing and bodyboarding weren't even on her radar. But then, neither was living in Costa Rica.

Dean chuckled. "They'll be pros in no time. All right. I'm going to hang up now and call the others. Let me know your itinerary and if anything changes."

"Will do." Max's thumb hovered over the icon to end the call. "Talk to you soon. Thanks, Dean."

"Yep."

After they hung up, Max dropped the phone on the bed and turned to face her. "Well, at least everyone will be vigilant now. I'll feel better once we're down there, though."

So would she. It had already bothered her being so far away from the kids. But now that she knew there was danger? She wanted to march straight to the nearest airport and fly a plane back to Costa Rica herself.

Her face crumpled. A soft sob escaped, and she covered her mouth, wavering on her feet. She so very much wanted to hug her babies.

Max's arms went around her, and she leaned into his warmth, grateful he was there to hold her together.

"Hey. None of that. They'll be fine. And look at it this way. Having the marshals there will give Emily someone new to terrorize."

Unbidden, a chuckle escaped. Sniffing, she eased back and wiped at her face. "We can break out the foam swords you bought and tell her they want to be her new sparring part-ners." She chuckled again, getting a hold of the fear that had momentarily overwhelmed her. The marshals would never know what hit them.

Max grinned. "That's a good plan. I think Marshal Marc-hand should be first. It can be comeuppance for keeping you in the dark."

Her brows knit together. "I agree." That angered her almost as much as Tad's deception.

Tipping her chin up, he placed a gentle kiss on her lips, further banishing the fear.

"Come on." Stepping back, he held out a hand. "Let's get packed up. I want to get downstairs and get our flight details from Marchand. See if I can change our seats." His nose wrinkled, making Margot chuckle again.

"You really don't like flying coach."

A roguish smile crossed his face. "Nope."

TWENTY-SIX

The soft thud of the car door shutting broke the nighttime stillness as Margot got out of Ford's car in Dean and Annabeth's driveway. Behind her, Marshal Marchand's headlights shut off as he cut the engine to his rental car. The man hadn't been happy when she and Max decided to ride with Ford and not with him. But she was with Max on this. The marshals could stay in the background. She trusted Ford and the others much more than any federal agents. They would never keep anything important from her. She also knew they'd lay down their lives to protect her children.

The exterior light on Dean and Annabeth's house blinked on. A moment later, the front door opened and Annabeth stepped into the doorway, a welcoming smile on her face. Dean stood behind her and off to the side. A bit of wariness entered Annabeth's gaze as she glanced past Margot at Marshal Marchand, but it was quickly snuffed out as Margot climbed the porch steps and enveloped her friend in a hug.

"Welcome back." Annabeth hugged her tight, then pulled back. "Did you have a good flight?"

"Max and I did. I don't know about Marchand." She

glanced back as she stepped into the house. "Max refused to sit in coach, so he bought the two of us first-class seats."

Amusement danced in Annabeth's eyes as Max stepped through the doorway, carrying their bags. "Why do you have to be difficult?"

Max grinned. "I wasn't. I just wanted to be comfortable. It's a long flight."

"It's not that long." Marchand appeared in the doorway. Ford walked in behind him.

"Long enough." Max set their bags down in the corner of the living room. "Annabeth, Dean, this is Marshal Kyle Marchand. Marshal, Dean and Annabeth Adler."

Marchand held out a hand. "Nice to meet you both."

Margot rocked back on her heels, waiting impatiently while the three shook hands. "Where are the girls?"

"Sleeping," Annabeth said. "Amy and I wore them out today. We took them and Gretchen to the beach again. I spent most of the time supervising Em on the bodyboard we borrowed from Edie."

Margot sighed, then smiled as she caught sight of Max's grin. He was right. She needed to get the girl her own board. Soon.

"The other two played in the water, built sandcastles, and collected shells for hours. Both twins barely made it through bath time and dinner before they fell asleep."

"I'm going to peek in on them." She pointed toward the hallway.

Annabeth nodded.

On light feet, Margot hurried down the hall to the guest room. Mindful of creaky door hinges, she gently opened the door and tiptoed inside. A nightlight plugged into the wall illuminated the room enough for her to see the two small forms curled up under the blankets on the queen-size bed.

The soft scuff of feet drew her attention to the door. Max

stepped in and came up behind her. He wrapped his arms around her, drawing her into his chest, and rested his chin on her shoulder. She leaned against him, soaking in the feel of his warm, masculine frame surrounding her, and covered his crossed arms with a hand.

"Even in sleep, their personalities are evident," he whispered.

Margot smiled. It was true. Lily slept on her side, knees bent, and one hand tucked under her pillow. Emily laid on her back, arms above her head and the blanket pulled down around her waist. Blonde hair fanned out around her head.

For several long moments, they stood there and watched the girls sleep. Margot wanted to touch them, but didn't dare. If either of them woke, it would wake the other, then it would be hours before they went back to sleep. She could wait until morning to hug and kiss all over them. For now, she was content to see them and know they were happy and safe.

Max stepped back and touched her waist. He tipped his head toward the door.

With one last glimpse, Margot followed him out of the room.

"So, what's the plan?" she asked as they rejoined the others. Two more men she didn't recognize now stood in the living room.

Ford and Dean shared a look before Ford glanced at Marchand. "The marshals are going to check into their hotel," he said. "Tomorrow, we'll move you and the girls to Max's house. Between its security, us hanging around, and the marshals on a rotation on the perimeter, you should be safe."

"Okay, what about tonight?" Margot said.

"Our house isn't really big enough for you two to stay," Dean said. "But since yours is right behind us, we thought that would be a good option. It'd keep you close to Em and Lily and not spread us too thin."

"And for the record"—Marchand held up a finger—"after we check into a hotel, I'll be back to help with security. I put in a request to have one more agent sent down so we can work in teams of two. My boss is working on finding us someone. We're stretched a little thin right now, so whoever it is will have to come from another office."

"Sounds good." Max put a hand in the middle of Margot's back. "We're going to leave you all to hash out the details of that. Someone can fill us in tomorrow morning. It's been a long day for us." Stepping away from her, he picked up their bags.

Margot wanted to sag in relief. She'd been dreading having to sit around and listen to them work out a security detail plan or answer more questions. Despite the bigger, more comfortable first-class seat, she hadn't slept on the way down. Her body was feeling the exhaustion. All she wanted to do was go to bed.

Giving Annabeth another hug, Margot let Max usher her out of the house and across the yards to her little cottage. She unlocked the door, stepping inside and flipping on the lights.

Max relocked the door behind them.

"Do you want the shower first?" she asked.

"No. You can go ahead. I'm going to find some bedding and make up the couch."

Glancing past him at the sofa, she bit her lip. It wasn't a two-seater, but it wasn't full-size, either. "Are you sure you want to sleep there? You can go home. I'll be fine by myself."

"Babe, I'm not going anywhere." He waved a hand toward the bathroom. "Go take your shower."

She could tell by the firm note in his voice, nothing she said would persuade him to leave. And honestly, she didn't want him to. His presence helped calm some of her anxiety about the danger directed at her and her daughters. Bottom line, Max made her feel safe.

"All right. The extra sheets and stuff are in the closet in the hallway. You can grab a pillow off my bed."

He nodded once and set their bags down by the kitchen island.

Margot retreated before she did something dumb and invited him to sleep with her. They'd kissed and skimmed the subject of a relationship, but that would be jumping several crucial steps. Like dating.

Ducking into her bedroom, she dug some fresh pajamas out of a drawer, then locked herself in the bathroom. Hot steam filled the room as the shower heated. She stripped out of her clothes and stepped into the spray.

The warm water relaxed her muscles. It also brought down some of the barriers in her mind. All the "what ifs" that had been safely locked up now swirled around.

What if Berry showed up?

What if their security measures failed?

What if they didn't?

What if *Tad* showed up?

It was that last one that bothered her most right now. She'd had time to think about the danger, but she hadn't let herself dwell too much on the fact Tad was alive. Mostly because she wasn't sure how she felt about that. About him.

She didn't love him anymore. Not the way she used to. He'd killed that love when he left without an explanation. When he left their daughters without a father.

Grabbing the shampoo bottle, she soaped her hair.

But she cared about him. She didn't wish him harm. Except for maybe a punch or two to the face and a good knee to the groin for all he'd done. One solid right hook to the nose, followed by a swift kick in the balls. She'd always considered herself a lady, and a rather proper one at that, but Max would probably have to hold her back if Tad showed up now.

A pair of smiling blue eyes flashed through her mind.

Max…

He was another "what if."

What if she let herself love again?

She could so easily love that man. She wasn't so sure she didn't already.

And really, what reasons did she have to not have a relationship with him? Their age difference? She didn't see that anymore. He was just Max.

Their friendship?

She could see that becoming a problem if they *didn't* do something about the way they felt.

Because those feelings weren't going away. They were only getting stronger.

Margot looked toward the door through the shower curtain. Max was out there making up a bed on a couch where the seat was about a foot too short for his frame to comfortably stretch out on.

He didn't have to.

She could invite him into her bed.

Soap sluiced over her shoulders and down her body as she rinsed her hair and contemplated that idea. The memory of their heated exchange at the hotel before Asher interrupted them sent a hot flush over her body. Could they just pick up where they'd left off that evening?

It was insane. She'd just told herself it was too soon.

But was it really? Considering how long they'd known each other? How well they knew each other?

The flush on her body turned into a fire that burned into her bones at the thought of Max's hands on all the places the water currently touched.

She wanted that.

Needed it.

Was that enough to throw caution to the wind and change everything?

TWENTY-SEVEN

A quick puff of steam billowed out behind Margot as she stepped out of the bathroom. Her gaze darted toward the living room. Max glanced up.

He'd removed his shoes and made up the sofa while she'd showered. She liked that he was comfortable in her home.

He stood and crossed the room, his footfalls silent in his stocking feet.

Stopping in front of her, he arched an eyebrow, his silvery blue gaze roving over her. Something sparked in his eyes, setting them ablaze.

She shivered, but not from a chill. If he'd physically touched her, she wasn't sure she'd have felt it more than that quick perusal.

"You don't look any more relaxed than when you went in there," he said. "I figured it would make you sleepy."

Sleep was now the furthest thing from her mind. Tingles raced from one end of her body to the other and back again. "No. My mind did the opposite. It woke up."

"That sucks. I'm sorry." He scrunched his nose, giving him an adorableness she couldn't resist.

She stepped closer, done keeping a leash on her feelings for this man. "I'm not." Snaking her hands up his shoulders, she combed her hands into his hair, loving the feel of the cool strands on her fingertips.

He must have seen the intention in her eyes, because he curled his hands over her hips. Margot bit her lip as his fingers dug into her flesh.

She'd been wrong. She could feel it more.

"Margot—"

She laid a finger over his lips. "Don't talk me out of it, Max. I know it's too soon; that we've barely talked about starting something more. But I—"

He ducked away from her finger and swallowed her words with a fierce kiss.

With a moan, she sank into him, letting go of the last thoughts rambling around in her head and just let herself feel.

His mouth glided over hers. He nipped and soothed as he went, dragging another moan from the depths of her soul. It was crazy, but she needed him like she needed air to breathe. If he stopped now, she'd wither up and expire.

Luckily, he seemed to be of the same frame of mind. Keeping their mouths fused, he tunneled his hands beneath the soft sweater she'd put on, searing her skin with his touch.

A soft gasp escaped her as his hands closed around her breasts. His callous-roughened palms raked over her sensitive flesh.

Like striking a match, the fire ignited in a flash.

One hand reversed direction, sliding around her torso and down her back, throwing gasoline on the fire as it burrowed under the waistband of her sleep shorts.

A wicked smile toyed with Margot's lips as every muscle in his body froze when he met with nothing.

She hadn't forgotten her underwear; she'd just chosen not

to go back into her room to get a pair when she realized she hadn't grabbed clean ones.

It never occurred to her that it would matter. Not even when she stepped out of the bathroom with the intention of doing this very thing. She'd been too nervous to worry about what she was or wasn't wearing.

But she was happy now she'd forgotten them. His reaction was everything.

She stood on her toes, pressing closer and urging him to keep going and touch her where her body burned the hottest for him.

Like she'd flipped a switch, he plunged his hand lower, skimming her center from behind. Margot moaned and squirmed in his hold, desperate for more.

Max ripped his mouth from hers, burying it in her neck. "You're killing me, Margot. Why aren't you wearing underwear?"

She couldn't answer. Not when that magical mouth was busy discovering that spot on her neck that drove her wild. She raked her hands through his hair, holding him to her. His fingers teased her once more, coaxing her body to ripen.

With a louder moan, she pushed on his shoulders, breaking his hold. Taking his hand, she turned and led him down the short hallway to her bedroom.

He pushed the door shut behind them.

Margot flipped on the small lamp on the bedside table, bathing them in its soft, warm glow. Her breath caught at the intense glitter in his now steely-blue eyes.

He stalked forward the few steps separating them, crowding her against the bed. She sat down, then crawled backward as he followed her onto the mattress. Hands gliding up her sides, he rucked her shirt up, exposing her to his hot gaze.

Her eyes nearly rolled out of her skull when he caught the

tip of her breast between his teeth. Strangling a groan, she clenched her fingers in his hair.

Max eased back. His heated gaze roved over her flushed cheeks and disheveled appearance.

She returned his hot stare.

This was insanity.

But she didn't want to stop. This storm had been brewing for months. Like an ocean current warming with the seasons to form a hurricane, all the little touches and heated glances, the quiet conversations and shared jokes had led them to this.

Margot whisked her shirt over her head.

His nostrils flared.

Lying back, she hooked her thumbs in the waistband of her shorts. His fingers tangled with hers, and they quickly went the way of her shirt. Drunk on the look in his eyes, she laid before him, naked and unashamed. He wanted her and liked what he saw, and she knew it.

It was hard not to when his pupils looked like those of a cat on the prowl.

He rose, taking two steps to stand just inches away.

Those lovely blue eyes took in everything. And they said everything he was powerless to speak.

For several long seconds, he stared at her. Bringing a hand up, he ghosted the backs of his fingers over the top of her knee and up her thigh.

Tingles raced the length of her leg and up her spine. Margot felt her nipples bead.

Easing down again, he took hold of the back of her neck and fused their mouths once again.

The room spun as he banded an arm around her waist and scooted her up the bed to the stack of pillows in a tangle of limbs.

"You're chilly." He ran a hand down her thigh.

She didn't feel the chill. Only the heat he'd created in her core.

"Let's warm you up, shall we?" A wicked smile tilted one side of his mouth as he sat up.

The question forming in her mind about how he planned to do that died a swift death as he shimmied down her body and pushed her legs open.

"I guess it's okay to eat a late-night snack before bed, right?" Leaning forward, he delved in.

Margot couldn't stop the shout that broke free as his tongue touched her. She grabbed a handful of his hair, not sure whether to push him away so she could breathe or hold on so he could send her to the heavens.

Her body made the decision for her.

The sensations were too much. Too good. She held him in place as he coaxed wave after wave of intense pleasure out of her. Once more, her shout echoed off the walls of the room.

Lethargy took over her muscles. Her fingers loosened in his hair, and he sat back. Climbing off the bed, he stripped out of his shirt and kicked out of his jeans, boxers, and socks.

Margot licked her lips as she got her first glimpse of the part of him she'd only ever dreamed about. And there had been dreams. Only a few, and they'd been recent. But they were enough to leave her wondering what hid behind the zipper of his jeans and how good it could make her feel.

Some of the mellowness left her body. Her core tightened once more in anticipation of what was to come. She sat up, sliding off the bed to take him in her mouth and give him some of the same pleasure he'd given her.

He let her play for all of two seconds before he hooked his hands under her arms and pulled her to her feet.

"I'm not young enough for you to do that and still have anything left for the main event."

She couldn't even pout before he guided her down to the bed and melded their bodies.

Stars danced in Margot's vision as they moved together, creating a delicious friction. She wound her legs around his waist and held on.

This was better than any dream could ever be.

The stars grew brighter until they blocked out the room and the sight of Max moving above her. She closed her eyes against the onslaught, but the light simply exploded behind her eyelids with the force of an atomic bomb. Margot let out a wild cry, bucking against him as pleasure ripped through her.

A moment later, his low grunt and hoarse moan joined her voice.

Sweaty, and breathing heavily, her limbs went limp. With a soft thump, her legs dropped to the bed.

His quiet curse brought some starch back to her bones. She opened her eyes.

Max stared down at the junction of their bodies, a look of trepidation on his handsome face.

She felt it the moment he looked up. The sticky wetness coating the inside of her thighs.

They'd just forgotten the most important lesson of middle school health class.

Margot covered her face and groaned.

"Hey." Max's hand enveloped hers, pulling her fingers away. "The chances are slim, right? People forget all the time and don't always get pregnant."

She did some quick math in her head.

A sharp laugh slid free. *Oh, this was bad.*

His shoulders fell. "We're in trouble, aren't we?"

She nodded.

"Um. Okay. We have options. They make a medication you can take, don't they? To"—he flip-flopped a hand—"undo our idiocy? Can we get that here?"

"I'm not sure, but even if they do sell it, I don't want to take that." She wasn't opposed to it, but there were worse things than being pregnant with Max's baby.

Relief flooded his face. "Good."

Surprise stilled her movements. "You... don't mind if I get pregnant from this?"

"Honestly?" He shifted, laying down on his side to her right. Sliding a hand up her arm, he brushed a lock of her hair back from her shoulder and stared at her collarbone for a long moment.

His eyes met hers, a vulnerability shining in their depths she'd never seen from him before. "I'd be elated if you get pregnant."

Twenty-Eight

Max couldn't believe he'd let himself get so swept away. It never once crossed his mind that they needed protection. When he'd slipped his hand into her pants and discovered her bare butt cheek, rationality evaporated. Every animal instinct he had came out to play, and his only thought had been how quickly he could get inside her.

But he wasn't mad about it. Apprehensive, sure. Especially with her initial reaction. But at his age, he'd given up hope of ever being a dad.

Margot blinked at him, her blue eyes wide. "Why?"

He rolled away to sit up. "Hang on." This conversation could take a bit, and he didn't want to be sticky for it. He doubted she did, either.

Getting up, he went to the bathroom and washed quickly, then wet a clean rag with warm water and brought it out to her. They needed a shower, but this would do for now.

Once he'd taken care of her, he put the rag on the night-stand and climbed in beside her, tugging the blankets over them.

"Are you going to tell me now why the possibility of us

having a baby makes you happy?" She'd curled into his side, using his shoulder as a pillow.

Max toyed with the ends of her hair and drummed his fingers on his chest as he stared up at the ceiling. "Have any of the guys mentioned my past?"

"Your past? Just your military stuff. I think one of them alluded to a relationship you had once. Is that what this is about?"

"Yeah. I was engaged once. A long time ago. Her name was Lotte. She was beautiful. And exotic. Our relationship was a whirlwind. We met at a bar in Italy when I was stationed there. I was young and dumb and enamored with this—vision— who'd taken a shine to me. I let her seduce me, and the next thing I knew, she was shoving a positive pregnancy test under my nose."

Margot shifted, propping up on an elbow to look at him. "Did she abort it?"

"No. She wanted the baby. I did too. I thought I had it all, you know? A great career. A beautiful Italian woman at my side. A baby on the way." He rolled his eyes, remembering the conversation he overheard with Lotte and her best friend.

"It wasn't yours, was it?"

"No. She was pregnant when we met. Anyway, before I knew all that, I proposed, thinking the baby was mine. We'd been engaged about four months when I came home from work for lunch. She was out in the garden with her best friend, Carla. I'd picked up enough Italian to realize they were talking about me and the baby."

"They didn't hear you coming?"

"No. You couldn't see the front door from the patio, and I didn't call out to her when I came in. It only took a few moments of listening to realize Carla was surprised I wasn't questioning the baby's size. Lotte wouldn't let me come to any of her appointments, saying that was how they did it in Italy." He lifted a shoulder. "I didn't have any Italian friends with kids to know any different. She told Carla I thought everything was normal. Then Carla asked how she planned to explain the baby being full term in size even though it would be six weeks earlier than I was expecting. Her answer? Gestational diabetes."

"Oh, Max." She laid a hand on his chest.

He covered it, linking their fingers. "I listened a little longer. Carla asked if she'd heard from Giacomo. Lotte laughed and said it didn't matter if he came around again or not. He'd served his purpose." Twenty years later, he could still feel the rage that had coursed through his blood. And the sadness. In an instant, she'd dashed his dreams.

"I couldn't hold my tongue after that. I stepped into view, and she knew from the second she saw my face that I heard everything. When I asked her why she'd do that, she said she did it so she could see the world."

Margot's eyes rounded. "She got pregnant and faked who the baby daddy was so she could travel? Did she not realize she'd have to take care of a child while she did that?"

"I don't know. I didn't ask that question. All I cared about was that she lied to me. I told her we were done, then went inside to pack."

"Did she try to stop you?"

"Briefly. She followed me into the bedroom and tried to use her body to convince me to stay. But she disgusted me now. She'd used me—used Giacomo and the innocent life they created—for her own gain."

He inhaled a deep breath, letting go of the anger that always simmered to the surface when he thought about Lotte. "After I left, I went and stayed with a friend from base. Luckily, I got deployed a few weeks after I moved out. My friend enlisted a few others to get the rest of my stuff while I was gone. A few months after that, my stint in Aviano was up, and I went back to the U.S."

"Did she ever try to contact you?"

"A couple of times. But I never answered the door or returned her calls. Then I left the country, and she had no way of doing so. I did hear from a friend, though, that she snagged some poor bastard and got married a month before the baby came. I don't know if it was the faceless Giacomo or some other sap. I just hope whoever it was gave that kid a good life." That was his only regret in the situation. He hadn't just left Lotte. But he couldn't be a father to a child that wasn't his when he didn't love or trust the mother. It was a recipe for failure.

"After I left Italy, I swore off women for a long time. I'd go out with buddies and drink and have a good time, but I never went home with anyone, never dated. I'd flirt, but that was all I wanted. It took a couple of years before I was ready for more. Even then, I kept things light. I just wasn't interested in a commitment."

"Is that why you're not married?"

"Mostly. That and I never found anyone who made me want to trust them with everything." He turned an intense stare on her. "Until you showed up. I've waited a long time to feel about a woman the way I feel about you. So, no. I'm not upset if we created a new life today." He held up a finger. "Just to be clear, that was not my intention. I lost my head, and for that I'm sorry. It's put you in a position you shouldn't be in."

Margot's wide-eyed stare lightened as she smiled. "I was an active participant, and you weren't the only one acting out of character."

He tipped his head. "True. But I still should have made sure to protect you. That's never happened to me before."

"Me, either." She rolled and stacked her hands on his

chest, resting her chin on top. "So, what do we do now? Not just about what could be, but about us?"

Max extended a hand and traced her cheekbone, brushing back a lock of her hair. "I'm not sure. Whatever we want, I suppose. But I can tell you I don't want to go backward. I don't want to just be your friend anymore, Margot."

"I don't think I want that, either. I guess we try this, right?" She arched an eyebrow. "See if we can make it work?"

"I think we have to. Above all else, I don't want to lose you. Not even as a friend. If we don't try, things will be awkward. And if we try, and give it everything and it ends, then I think we can agree we weren't meant for more. That we're suited best as friends."

His gaze dropped to the dark hollow and the pillowy softness of the tops of her breasts. He felt his body tighten. "Though considering what just happened and how I already want it to happen again, I don't think that'll be the case."

A slow, seductive smile spread over her lips and her bright blue eyes darkened to a deep midnight. "No. I think we're destined to be much more than friends."

Pushing up on her hands, she threw a leg over his hips. "So, just how long *does* it take for you to recover?"

Max gave a low chuckle. "I guess we're about to find out."

Twenty-Nine

"You ready for this?" Margot glanced over her shoulder at Max as they neared Dean and Annabeth's back door. "We're about to get attacked."

He grinned. "Bring it on. I've missed the rug rats."

A bright smile wreathed her face, and she reached for the doorknob. That was another thing she loved about Max. He truly loved and adored her children.

Surreptitiously, she touched her belly. Would they soon add another little one to the mix?

Nerves churned in her stomach, but so did excitement. She wasn't nervous about having a child with Max. She already knew he'd make a great dad. That he'd stick around and raise their baby. It was more the drastic change to her life a new baby would bring.

She didn't know why that made her nervous. Changes were coming with or without a baby.

Stepping inside, two blonde heads swung toward her from where the twins sat at the table eating breakfast. It only took a second for the girls to recognize who was here.

Chairs scraped the floor amidst a chorus of "Mommy!

Mommy's home!" In moments, Margot had both girls in her arms.

On her knees, she hugged them tight. Burying her face in Lily's hair, she closed her eyes and took a deep breath, letting the girl's scent wash over her. All the stress and worry from the last few days evaporated.

Kissing their cheeks, she rose, holding them both.

Emily turned and saw Max. With a wide smile, she reached for him.

Grinning, he took the girl and placed a smacking kiss on her cheek. "How's my girl? Were you good for Dean and Annabeth?"

She nodded. "We went surfing!"

"I heard. Later, you'll have to show me how good you are." He looked at Lily. "Both of you."

Margot nodded. "I want to see too. Right now, you two need to finish your breakfast." She set Lily on the floor. "Then we're going to Max's house."

Emily's little fist shot up as Max set her down. "Yes! Swimming! Lily! We get to go swimming!" She scampered back to the table and hopped into her chair.

Chuckling, Margot shook her head. "Good to know my absence didn't dampen her spirit. Or her love of swimming."

Dean snorted. "I don't think anything could kill that. That kid's a fish."

"Probably not," Max agreed.

Margot glanced around, then out the front window. "Where are our marshal friends?"

"Outside, somewhere," Dean said. "Marchand went to the hotel in the middle of the night to get some sleep. One of the others, Beale, relieved him. Ford and Sam switched places too."

"Did you get any rest?" Margot frowned at the man. Dark circles rimmed his eyes.

"Some. I woke up when Ford and Sam switched spots. They stayed in the house until the girls got up. Sam's outside now with the marshal."

"Do we know any more today than we did last night? About where Berry is?" Max propped his hands on his hips.

"Not that I know of. But I haven't talked to the marshals since we went to bed." Dean's phone rang as he finished talking. Reaching into his pocket, he withdrew it. A crease formed on his forehead. "It's Asher." He slid his thumb over the screen and answered, but didn't put it on speaker in deference to the little ears only feet away.

Margot crossed her arms and resisted the urge to tap her foot while she waited to hear what Asher had to say. When Dean's eyebrows shot up, her heart rate followed. She clutched her shirtsleeves, hoping he hung up soon and filled them in.

A minute later, he said goodbye and pocketed his phone.

"Well?" Max rolled a hand when Dean didn't immediately relay what Asher said.

Mouth flat, Dean's gaze traveled between him and Margot.

A pit formed in her stomach. "What?"

"Asher figured out how Dale Conroy's connected to the case. He was a patient of Tad's. Considering that the body you found is likely Conroy and the money from the bank robbery was found on his farm, it's highly likely Tad killed him."

Bile rose in her throat. She didn't want to believe it. The man she'd married wasn't capable of murder.

Or so she'd thought. She was beginning to think she never truly knew the real Tad Gaultier.

Max walked to the door.

"What are you doing?" Dean asked.

"Finding Marchand." He yanked the door open and stepped outside.

A moment later, Margot heard him bellow the marshal's name.

The twins' chatter at the table stopped. They both turned to stare at the door. Margot moved over to them, pinning a happy smile on her face. She wasn't surprised they were shocked at the sound. They'd never heard Max raise his voice quite like that before.

As much as she wanted to stay and be part of the conversation, she needed to get the girls out of here. This was not something they needed to be part of, and she trusted Max to fill her in later.

"Are you guys done?"

Two small faces turned up to look at her. Lily nodded.

"Good. Go find your shoes, please."

Both girls climbed off their chairs and scampered toward the back door. Margot glanced at the front of the house and the open front door. Max was out of sight.

The twins returned, shoes in hand. Margot knelt in front of them to help them put on the sandals. She was strapping the last strap on Emily's shoe when Max walked back in with Marchand and Sam. Audra was with them too.

Relief flooded Margot's veins. She'd been prepared to hijack Annabeth's car and drive to Max's house alone. But there were enough people here, someone with some training could accompany her and watch her back.

Walking into the throng, she took Max's hand and pulled him aside.

"Everything okay?" A concerned frown marred his forehead.

"The girls don't need to be here for this."

His frown intensified. "I'm sorry. I didn't mean to startle them. I'm just—" He broke off with a growl, raising a hand and curling his fingers into a fist. His jaw worked.

"I know." She pulled his hand down and threaded their fingers together.

He sighed. "Um, I'll take you home. The guys—"

"No. You stay. I want one of us to stay informed. One of the others can take us."

"I'll take them." Audra stepped forward, having overheard their conversation. "Sam can update me later."

"I'll go too," Annabeth said. "This"—she waved a hand at her husband and the others—"is not really my thing."

"Are you sure?" Max asked.

"Yes." Audra turned to Emily and Lily. "Girls, let's get your things." She held out a hand, ushering the twins toward the hallway and the bedroom they'd been using.

Margot looked at Max again.

He framed her face in his palms. "You be careful. Eyes in the back of your head, all right? If anything seems weird—"

She covered his hands and stood on her toes to kiss him and stop the flow of words. "We'll be okay," she whispered.

Tiny voices grew louder as Audra and the twins returned. Margot stepped back. Giving Max a tremulous smile, she turned her attention to her daughters. "You guys ready to go?"

"Yep! I wanna swim!" Em raised her fists.

"Then let's go swim."

The girls traipsed toward the door. At the threshold, Lily turned back and frowned when she saw Max wasn't following her mother and Audra.

"Let's go, Max."

"I'll be there a little later, sweetie. But you have fun swimming, okay?"

Her little frown remained for another moment before she nodded. Her eyes traveled over the adults, lingering on Marchand.

Margot had a feeling the little girl understood far more than she should.

Her little perceptive child.

Thirty

Max ran a hand through his hair and gripped the back of his neck, watching Margot and the girls disappear through the door. Reality had crashed down hard this morning, popping the bubble they'd created last night. He wanted to go back to it. Nothing would please him more than to go about his day playing in the pool with those two sweet girls, then later, loving on their mama again in hopes of giving them a sibling.

"You all right?" Sam asked.

"Yeah." Max dropped his hand. He looked at the marshal. "Marchand, tell me you know where Berry is."

The marshal's mouth twisted. "I wish I could. And now that your contact discovered Conroy's connection to things, I don't have any leads to go on to find him."

A dark frown transformed Max's face. He glared at Marchand. "We need Tad. He's the only one left who can give us any insight into Berry."

Marchand's mouth flattened, and he glanced away. Max could see the hesitation on his face.

"I'm not really asking, Marshal. If you don't call him and loop him in, we *will* find him and do it ourselves."

The marshal's expression sharpened. "I'll have you arrested."

Sam snorted. "You can try. But you'll never be able to prove it was us."

A mirthless smile appeared on Dean's face. "It's true. All you'll discover is that it was an *anonymous tip*."

Marchand muttered a curse and scrubbed his hands over his face. "I truly hate your little group. Dye was right. You all are impossible."

Max flashed him a quick, toothy smile. "Glad we've cleared that up. So, who's making the phone call? You or me?"

Blowing out a breath, Marchand aimed an annoyed look at him. "I will."

"Good. We want to listen in," Dean said. "To make sure you tell him the whole truth."

"The whole—" Marchand stopped with an exasperated sigh, then pinched the bridge of his nose. He waved his hand. "Fine."

Max crossed his arms, waiting.

Marchand's brows rose. "You mean, right now?"

"Yes."

"Christ almighty," Marchand muttered under his breath. He removed his phone from his pocket. Clicking through several screens, he finally dialed a number and put it on speaker.

It rang five times, then rolled to voicemail.

Max clenched his teeth. *Dammit.*

Marchand left a quick message, asking Tad to call, then hung up. "Happy? That's all I can do for now."

"Where is he?" Sam asked.

Again, Marchand hesitated.

Max huffed. "We've been over this. No information is safe. But it is quicker if you tell us."

"I think I need to have a chat with the FBI's cybersecurity team about your friend."

Dean chuckled. "Trust me, they're already aware of him. Answer Sam's question."

The marshal threw his hands up. "Fine. He's in California. North of San Francisco."

Max glanced at Dean, who already had his phone out to call Asher. In moments, ringing filled the living room.

"Yo. You talk to that marshal about what I told you?" Asher asked without preamble.

"We did. He's here, and you're on speaker."

"Got it. What's up?"

"Our new friend told us where he stashed Tad."

A beat of silence came over the line.

Max narrowed his eyes. "You already know, don't you?"

"Maybe." Asher drew out the word. "I might also have driven down there and talked to him yesterday."

"You did what?" Marchand stepped closer, glaring at the phone in Dean's hand. "You had no authority—"

"Can it, Marshal. The man's children are in danger. He has every right to know. Especially since he's the cause."

Marchand took a breath, closing his eyes. Max could tell he was counting to ten in his head.

"What did you say to him?" Marchand finally asked.

"Only what we know so far. That you found his car and a body up in North Dakota and that you called Margot in to make an identification. I also mentioned Conroy. He clammed up at that. That's what made me dig a little deeper into Tad's connections, which is how I found out Conroy was a patient. Anyway, he asked a few questions about Margot and the girls, then thanked me for telling him what the marshals wouldn't."

Max bit back a grin at the subtle dig.

"Then what?" Marchand asked.

"Then I went home."

Marchand muttered a curse.

"Do you have eyes on Tad?" Max glanced at Marchand.

"No. There's a marshal in the area in case he needs someone, and we have monitors on his credit cards and bank accounts as well as a GPS tracker in his car, but no one follows him around twenty-four-seven." He lifted his phone. "I need to make some calls."

"You do that." Max resisted the urge to roll his eyes. There were so many ways Tad could elude WitSec. All it would take would be a sympathetic friend or co-worker to give him a ride. Or even some cash. He could steal a credit card too. He'd already proven adept at covering his tracks. He could have another identity the marshals didn't know about.

Still frowning fiercely, Marchand went out the back door.

Max turned to his friends. "Asher, do you have any idea where Tad is?"

"No. But my best guess is he's on his way down there to you. I saw the panic in his eyes when I told him Margot was involved. Berry scares him."

That's what Max had been afraid of. Tad was bringing the danger to them. "All right. We'll keep an eye out for him."

"Good. I'll keep digging too. See if he pops up anywhere."

"Sounds good," Dean said. "Thanks."

"Yep. Talk to you later." Asher hung up.

"I don't like this," Sam said as soon as the line went silent. "It feels like everything is coming to a head. With Margot and the twins right in the crosshairs."

Max's jaw worked.

He agreed.

Thirty-One

W ater droplets sprayed Margot in the face as Em leaped off the diving board once again. She smiled and clapped her hands when the girl broke the surface and paddled her way toward the steps. Some of the stress perpetually plaguing her had evaporated watching the girls play. Their giggles and shouts of "Watch me, Mommy!" had filled her happiness well high enough to push back some of the negative emotions.

Legs appeared next to her, then a glass of tea with ice cubes clinking against the sides as Annabeth sat down on the pool deck.

"Here."

"Thanks." Margot accepted the glass and took a sip. It was warm today, even this early, so the cold tea felt delicious sliding down her throat.

"You're welcome." Annabeth took a sip from her glass, then watched the girls for a moment before speaking. "I couldn't help but notice that kiss you laid on Max. Things have changed between you two, I take it?"

A shy smile formed on Margot's face. She swiped at the

condensation on her glass. "Yeah. Quite a bit." She glanced at her friend. "We, um, got a little carried away and, well... I might be pregnant." Saying it out loud to someone else made it more real. And made her want it even more. If she wasn't, well, she and Max needed to have a discussion about making that a reality.

Annabeth's eyes grew round. "What? How certain are you?"

Margot tipped a hand back and forth. "The timing was right. I guess we'll know soon enough."

For several long moments, Annabeth stared at her. "You don't seem too concerned about it," she finally said.

"I'm not." A slow smile spread over her face. "We recognized the slip-up right away and talked about it. Surprisingly, we both hoped it would result in a baby. I'm ready, Annabeth. I want to move on. With Max."

"It's about damn time!"

Margot laughed. "I know. We've been stubborn, not wanting to ruin a good friendship. But it finally reached a point where the friendship would suffer if we *didn't* start something romantic."

Annabeth squealed, then hugged her quick. "I'm so stinking excited for you!"

"Why are we hugging?" Audra glided over, water rippling out behind her as she waded closer. They'd made a couple of quick stops for swimsuits before coming to Max's.

"Margot and Max finally gave in to what we've all known for months."

"Brilliant." Audra grinned. "When's the wedding?"

Chuckling, Margot smiled at her. "We haven't discussed marriage yet."

"But they've discussed babies." Annabeth added.

Audra tipped her head. "Makes sense. Max is old."

Margot rolled her eyes. "He's not that old. Trust me." A blush stole over her face, and she chuckled.

A buzzer from inside interrupted their laughter. Margot turned toward the sound. That was the buzzer for the front gate.

Audra heaved herself out of the pool, but Annabeth was already on her feet. She waved Audra back. "Stay. You're dripping. I'll check who it is."

Sitting down next to Margot, Audra nodded.

"Mommy! Watch!"

Margot glanced at the diving board to see Lily making her way to the end. She inched toward the edge, pausing for a second before leaping into the pool.

Margot clapped. Audra let out a loud whistle as Lily surfaced.

"Bang up job, Lil!" Audra said.

"You did so great, sweetie." Margot grinned. That was the first time Lily had worked up enough courage to jump off the diving board.

"I did, didn't I?" Lily made it to the side of the pool and clutched the edge. A wide, joyous smile on her face. "I'm gonna do it again!"

"Surfing must have been good for her confidence," Margot said to Audra.

"I think so. She's a lot more comfortable in the water."

"Margot. Aud. Come here."

Margot turned at the sound of Annabeth's voice from the back door. The serious note in it had her stomach doing flip-flops. "What is it?"

"Just... come here." She motioned them over.

Frowning, Margot turned to the twins. "Girls. Let's take a break from the pool for a few minutes, okay?"

Emily groaned, doggy-paddling in the deep end. "But I'm not done swimming."

"I know. But you need to hydrate. How about we go grab a popsicle?"

"Ooo, popsicles!" Lily scampered down the steps off the diving board. "I want a blue one!" She started to run toward the house.

"Walk, please," Margot reminded her as she got up and slipped on her shoes.

The girl's steps immediately slowed to a quick walk.

Audra leaned down and held out a hand to Emily. "Come on, poppet. What color lolly do you want?"

"Purple!" Like her sister, as soon as her feet hit the ground, she trotted toward the house, moving as fast as possible without running.

"Girls, let's dry off first." Margot snagged their towels from the chaise.

They paused long enough for her to wrap a towel around their shoulders, then they were off again, hurrying inside for their popsicles.

Once the twins had their treat and were dripping water onto the tiled kitchen floor at the table, Margot and Audra followed Annabeth into the living room to the video screen on the wall by the front door.

Not saying a word, Annabeth just pointed.

"What—"

Audra didn't get to finish. Margot's gasp cut her off.

Heart hammering in her chest—along with a healthy dose of anger, she looked at a wide-eyed Annabeth. "What's he doing here? How did he even find us?"

"I don't know. I told him to hang on a moment. It's been several. I'm surprised he's still there."

Margot wasn't. He was probably scared out of his mind.

Standing at the gate, practically melded into the foliage by the pillar and barely in view of the camera, was Tad.

THIRTY-TWO

The anger boiling in Margot's blood swiftly pushed out any surprise. Who the hell did he think he was showing up here after all this time? After all he'd done?

Reaching out, she yanked open the door and stepped through.

"Margot, wait." Audra's voice followed her outside.

"No. I'm done playing whatever game this is." She marched down the hill, shoes slapping against the asphalt driveway.

She heard Audra groan. "You could at least let me put on some shorts and grab my gun."

"He won't hurt me."

"It's not him I'm worried about."

The danger they were all facing penetrated the rage burning through her brain, and she halted just before they rounded the bend in the drive. With a huff, she turned. "Fine. Go. I'll wait here."

"How about you come back up with me?"

Margot crossed her arms. "You can sprint that distance

and back before I'd even make it to the house. I'm not running up this hill."

Audra rolled her eyes. "I'll be right back." Spinning around, she took off up the drive.

Sighing, Margot turned, glancing down the hill. She couldn't see the gate from here.

Was he still there? How long would he wait?

She crept forward, moving off the driveway. It wouldn't hurt to peek while she waited on Audra. Just to make sure he hadn't left.

Margot pushed into the trees and hedges lining the drive, thankful they lived in a jungle. Easing down the hill, she crept forward until she could see through the foliage.

From this angle, she couldn't see much. But the top of his dark blond head was visible.

Her anger surged again. He'd be lucky if she didn't slap him. Or punch him in the nose.

Max might. She wouldn't stop him. She'd probably cheer him on.

Leaning against a tree, she studied him, keeping one ear open for Audra's return. He looked good for a supposed dead man. Healthy. But he was twitchy. He couldn't stay still, she noticed. And every little sound drew his attention.

"Margot!" Audra's hissed exclamation drifted through the jungle.

She glanced over her shoulder, seeing the woman coming down the hill. Pushing off the tree, she emerged from the dense foliage near the gate.

"You scared me half to death." Audra leveled a fierce frown on her. "I thought something happened to you."

"Sorry. I wanted to make sure he didn't leave."

"We'd have found him. He couldn't get far around here. There's only one road in and out, and the guys are on their way. Annabeth called them as soon as we left the house."

"Well, at least we'd have known which way he went."

Audra just blinked.

Margot shrugged and started down the driveway. Together, they rounded the bend.

Tad noticed and backed up into the hedge before recognizing her. He eyed Audra warily.

"Hi." He lifted a hand and waved it once.

Margot and Audra stopped a few feet from the iron gate set into the stone pillars.

"What the hell do you want, Tad?" Margot crossed her arms and glared, virtually vibrating as she came face-to-face with the man who'd destroyed her life fourteen months ago.

He tipped his head back, looking skyward, then sighed. "Are the girls all right?"

"They're fine. Why are you here?"

"I just..." His mouth pulled. "It wasn't supposed to be this way, Margot." He blinked several times and looked away.

Margot sighed, some of her ire leaving. Now she was just pissed and disappointed. "I still don't understand why you're here. I mean, I get that you're concerned, but you could have called. Or, you know, come clean with me to begin with."

"I know. I handled all this terribly. But that doesn't matter now. I know you know what's going on. I talked to some friend of yours. Asher. I—I think Fred's here. I don't want him coming after you and the girls. It's me he wants."

Audra stepped to the side and hit the button to open the gate. Margot glanced at her with a curious frown.

"He's better off in here with us. I have questions, and the guys will too."

Lips pursed, Margot didn't argue. She didn't like it, but knew Audra was right. This wasn't a conversation to have at the end of the driveway. "Fine. But let's get one thing clear. The girls will not recognize you. When you walked out and gave up your rights to them, I erased you from our lives. I didn't want to give them false hope that you'd be back. And I still don't. So, as far as they're concerned today, you're just an old friend who's come to visit."

Hurt flashed in his eyes, but he nodded. "I understand. I never wanted to hurt them. Or you. I was trying to protect you."

Margot's jaw worked, some of her anger returning. "There were better ways." Spinning on her heel, she set off back up the drive.

When she reached the front door, she hesitated and glanced back. "I meant what I said. They don't need to know who you are."

"I won't say anything, Margot. I promise. I get it. You're right. I won't be able to be here for them. They don't deserve that kind of dad."

Max's face flashed through her mind. He was the kind of dad she wanted for her daughters. She had no doubt Tad loved Emily and Lily, but Max did, too, and he would never leave.

Turning around, she let them into the house.

The living room was empty.

"Annabeth?" Margot called.

Tad groaned.

She looked at him as she walked toward the kitchen. His shoulders had slumped, and he now had a look of dismay written on his face.

"I was hoping to avoid her. I thought that was her voice on the intercom. She's going to filet me like a fish."

Margot didn't bother to hide her smile. "Most likely. But for now, you're safe. She won't do it in front of the twins."

Only a modicum of relief crossed his face.

They entered the kitchen to find it empty. A quick glance outside showed Emily back on the diving board. She dashed down it and jumped into the pool. Lily climbed the steps, watching for her sister to swim out of the way.

"God, they've gotten so big." Emotion thickened his voice.

Margot swallowed around the lump in her throat. She felt for him. He'd missed a lot and would miss even more. But it was his own doing.

"Stay here," Audra said. "It might be best if you watch through the window." She walked toward the door. "I'll let Annabeth know we're back."

Margot nodded, then she was gone.

Tad moved closer to the window, staring out at the pool. "Lily's still cautious, I see."

The girl moved at a much more sedate pace toward the end of the diving board before jumping off the end.

"They're both great swimmers, though," he remarked.

"They spend a lot of time here."

"Is this the British lady's house?"

"No. It belongs to my partner."

"Partner?" He glanced back, a frown creasing his brows.

"Max Carson. We're dating."

"Oh." He nodded. "I think I saw him. I hid across the street from your house when I first arrived. He's the one you went home with last night, right?"

Twin pops of color heated her cheeks, and her eyes turned hard. "You were spying on me?"

He held up his hands. "Not like that. I went to your house when I got here, hoping to just catch a glimpse of you and the girls. To make sure you were safe. But you weren't back yet. So I sat in the bushes and watched. You showed up with Marchand and two men I don't know. Then I saw you go to your house with one of them. Was that him?"

Margot's expression remained sour, not liking that he'd been watching, and no one had known. It made her wonder who else could be out there. "Yes."

His head bobbed, and he turned to stare out at the twins

again, tucking his hands under his arms. "I hope he's a better partner and father than I was."

She kept her mouth shut. There was no point confirming or denying anything. He knew he'd screwed up and that she wouldn't fall for the same thing again, no matter how handsome the man.

"I really am sorry, Margot. About everything." He turned his head enough to see her from the corner of his eye. "From the gambling and the lies to how I left. I made a royal mess of things, and I just—I was ashamed to tell you what I'd done."

"I get that. But I was your wife. We vowed in good times and in bad. You should have trusted me—trusted our marriage—enough to confide in me."

"I know, but I couldn't bear to have you look at me like the loser I'd become."

"Tad, you're not a loser. You made mistakes."

He scowled, giving a soft huff. "Big ones." He shook his head. "Most of all, I just didn't want to look you in the eye and know that I'd hurt you." His gaze flicked to hers. "I know that makes me a coward. I'm so sorry, Margot."

She clenched her teeth, holding his gaze. Forgiving him wouldn't come easily, but she was glad he'd admitted his wrongdoings. "Thank you for apologizing."

"I know it won't erase it. And I don't expect you to forgive me. Not right away. But eventually, I'd like to have a relationship with them." He pointed out the window. "Whenever that may be. I'm still in a lot of trouble."

The skeletal remains she'd found on Conroy's farm entered her mind. She bit the inside of her cheek, holding back the questions. Marchand needed to be here for that.

THIRTY-THREE

Max barely waited for the car to come to a halt before he was out and charging up the walkway to his front door. He knew Tad wouldn't do anything to hurt Margot or the girls, but the thought of her facing her ex without him there to lean on—it bugged the crap out of him.

The quick staccato of the others' footsteps echoed behind him as he opened the door. His gaze traveled through the living room to the backyard. He could see Emily on the diving board. Audra stood to the side, her arms crossed, one eye on the pool and the other on the house.

"Margot?" His voice echoed through the cavernous room.

"Kitchen," came her reply.

He veered left, weaving around the furniture. Crossing the threshold, he stopped, his gaze going to the blond-haired man standing in front of the window.

Emily and Lily's eyes stared back at him from the man's face.

Max clenched his teeth. And his fists.

"Easy." Sam's hand landed on his shoulder.

He shrugged it off and crossed to Margot's side. Lifting a hand, he skimmed his knuckles over her face. "You all right?"

She nodded. Taking his hand, she laced their fingers together, then nodded at the man. "Max, this is Tad. Tad, Max. And that's Sam, Dean, and you know Marchand." She gestured around the half circle the men had formed, introducing them all.

Tad gave them all a tight smile. "Hello."

Marchand propped his hands on his hips. "Do I even want to know how you evaded the safeguards we had in place, or how you managed to get on an international flight without a problem?"

Tad wrinkled his nose. "Probably not. But it was for good reason. I think Fred's here."

The marshal's gaze sharpened.

Max's hand tightened around Margot's.

"What makes you say that?" Marchand asked.

"After that friend of theirs"—he nodded at the men and Margot—"came to talk to me, I called around to some... contacts. The consensus was that Fred had a line on how to get his money. Not a line on the *money*, but how to get it." He lifted a shoulder and glanced out the window. "There's only one thing that would get me to give up where I hid it."

Marchand gave a short huff through his nose. "I'm not even going to touch on you breaking WitSec protocol right now." He waved a hand. "Why did he wait so long? We know he knows who you really are. Owens knew, so it stands to reason Berry does too. Why would he wait all this time to come after your ex-wife and your kids?"

"Because Owens didn't tell him about them until recently. That's why Berry killed him. To keep him from going to the cops and stopping him." Tad ran a hand through his hair. "Devin was a bastard, but he wasn't evil. He drew the line at hurting people's families. He called me. Devin did. After Fred 'coaxed'"—he air-quoted—"the information out of him. And no, I don't know how he got my new number. Probably one of the people I'd kept in contact with. Anyway, after his call, I skipped out on the federal agents I was working with, packed up a bunch of my stuff, and hopped on a bus to Idaho. There, I bought a car."

Marchand held up a hand. "Where did you get the money to buy a car? I know what your finances look like. You don't have that much. Now or then."

Tad's gaze darted to Margot. Suddenly, Max knew what he'd done with some of the money he'd gotten from stealing her jewelry and coins.

"I had some savings you didn't know about," Tad said.

"Why did we find so much of your stuff in the car?" Margot asked.

"Because I took a lot with me. I wasn't certain I was going back to my new life. Turns out, I was right about that. Someone in Devin's organization turned on him and told Fred that Devin contacted me. We ran when he showed up at the apartment Devin and I rented in Boise."

He glanced at Marchand. "And before you ask, I didn't intend to leave my car and belongings behind the way I did. We spent a couple days driving through Montana and into North Dakota, but Fred's like a damn bloodhound. He tracked us down when we were in the Badlands. I'd let Devin drive that day, so he had the key when we got separated. When I couldn't find him again after several hours, I started looking for help. I ended up coming across an older couple who were driving through the park. I fed them some story about getting lost and asked for a ride to town. They were happy to oblige. From there, I caught another bus and went back to my WitSec house and pretended like nothing happened. I've kept a low profile since, hoping he wouldn't find me." His jaw worked. "Instead, he found my family."

"Did you try to contact Owens again?" Marchand asked.

"Yes. Eventually, his number stopped working. That's when I knew Fred had gotten to him."

"You should have come to me with this." Marchand pointed at his own chest. "We could have tracked Berry down. Stopped him from coming after you or your family."

Tad scoffed. "Yeah. Because the feds have done such a great job so far." He shook his head. "You had a year by then to nail Devin and Fred. With my help! And you couldn't do it. So, forgive me if I didn't have any faith you could keep them safe. I still don't."

A touch of admiration took the edge off Max's anger toward Tad. It seemed he wasn't an entirely selfish bastard.

Marchand speared him with a glare. "You also didn't tell us the whole truth. How about you start with Conroy?"

Tad's jaw worked. He glanced away. "I'd rather not."

Margot's fingers tightened. Max squeezed back, knowing she had to be hurting. Tad had as much as admitted to killing the old man.

Several beats went by as Marchand stared at Tad. "So, what was your plan coming here?" Marchand continued, apparently choosing not to press the issue for the moment.

"Find Berry before he could get to Margot or the kids. I figured if I hung around in the shadows, I'd see him coming."

"And do what?" Margot asked. "Let him take you instead of me or Em or Lily? None of those scenarios are acceptable."

"I wasn't going to let him take me. Or any of you." The hard glint in his eyes said what he didn't vocalize.

The muscles in Margot's jaw clenched, then she looked away.

Max let go of Margot's hand to run his up over her shoulder and rest at the back of her neck between her shoulder blades. He turned to his friends and Marchand. "We need a better plan than sit and wait."

"I'll check with the Costa Rican travel authorities," Marchand said. "Find out if he used his passport to get into the country."

"I doubt he did. There are a number of ways he could get down here without going through official channels," Max said.

"He's right," Sam added. "We need to set up a sting of some sort."

"Such as?" Marchand raised an eyebrow.

Sam tipped his head, looking at Tad. "You mentioned you still have some contacts from your previous life. Are these ones that know Berry?"

"Yes."

"You're going to call one you know would snitch and ask for help."

Tad frowned. "Help with what?"

"What you set out to do. Killing Berry."

Thirty-Four

"There. All done." Margot set the hairbrush down, having finished brushing out Lily's hair after her bath. "Go pick out a book."

The girl scampered out of the bathroom and down the hall to the room Max had set up for them months ago. It was outfitted with two twin beds, a mountain of toys, and a bookshelf filled with every children's book he'd been able to find. Margot had tried to protest when he did it. She didn't mind the idea of him having some toys and books in the house; they did spend a lot of time here. But he'd gone well over the top with their room. She'd convinced him to return some of the toys, but he'd put his foot down on the books, telling her more books were never a bad thing.

She couldn't argue with that, so her daughters now had a better library than she did.

Turning off the light, she left the bathroom and followed Lily down the hall. Emily was already in the bedroom, picking out her own book.

The scene on the floor by the bookshelves made her smile.

Max was in one of the oversize bean bags, Emily in his lap.

The book she'd chosen was open in front of them, but he'd paused to help Lily pick hers. She had two in her tiny hands and was holding them up for him to see.

Margot walked over, grabbing the second bean bag and dragging it close to his. She sat down, and Lily climbed into her lap with a book about kittens. Max flipped back a couple of pages and started Emily's book again, so Lily could hear it all.

Normally, once they finished their stories, Margot would pop both girls in bed and bid them goodnight. But tonight, she and Max wanted to talk to them. The girls were bound to notice how differently they treated each other, and she didn't want there to be any question about why.

So, when Lily tried to get up at the end of the book, Margot tightened her hold. "Hang on, sweetie. Max and I need to talk to you two."

The girl stilled and looked up.

"So, what would you say if we spent even more time with Max?"

"Swimming?" Em immediately asked.

Margot chuckled. "I'm sure there will be more swimming. But I meant more as like a family. Like Amy and Ezra with their daughter Gretchen."

"Like a daddy?" Lily asked.

Max met Margot's gaze. A slow smile spread over his face, happiness making his eyes shine.

"Yes," Margot said. While they hadn't made a hard and fast commitment to each other—no professions of undying love or proposals of marriage—becoming a family unit was the goal.

"I'd like a daddy," Em said. "Gretchen has a daddy. He's nice." She tipped her head back to spear Max with a look. "Will you take me to surfs?"

Max chuckled. "Of course I will. We'll do all kinds of stuff.

Just like we do now. Mostly, this means that we're all going to spend more time together and that I'm responsible for you guys, just like your mommy is. I hope one day soon you'll all move in here."

"Are you gonna get married, like Ann-beth and Dean?" Emily asked.

Max's gaze flicked to Margot's, and he smiled again. "If your mommy says yes when I ask her."

Emily's head turned to look at Margot. "Say yes. We want a daddy."

Margot laughed. "I don't think you'll have to worry about that." She clutched Lily close, pressing her cheek to the girl's damp hair as she gazed at Em. The emotion she'd been dancing around for months but never letting herself fully feel finally overflowed its well. She looked up at Max with a tremulous smile, unable to stop the words that spilled free. "I love Max very much."

The smile froze on his face and his eyes rounded. A moment later, the widest, happiest smile she'd ever seen on him brightened his expression.

"Yeah?" He tipped his head.

She nodded. "Yeah."

"I love you too." He held her gaze for a moment, then looked down at the girl in his arms, then Lily. "All of you."

Emily turned in his arms, standing up on his lap. She wrapped her little arms around his neck and pressed a kiss to his cheek. "I love you too."

Lily pushed out of Margot's lap and scrambled into Max's. "Me too!"

Tears swam in Margot's vision. She'd worried a bit how the girls would take the change in their relationship with him. She shouldn't have.

Max looked at her from between the twins, his bright smile now a little watery.

Emily pulled back. "I'm gonna call you Daddy Max."

A surprised chuckle slipped past his lips. "You are, huh?"

She nodded, her expression solemn. "Yep."

Lily looked back at Margot. "Mommy, can we play with Gretchen tomorrow? I want to tell her I have a daddy, now, too!"

Margot smiled at her daughter. "We might be able to arrange that. I'll call Amy in the morning, okay?"

"Okay!" Lily kissed Max's cheek, then turned and sat down. "Can we have another story, Daddy Max?"

He chuckled. "Sure. Which one do you want?"

THIRTY-FIVE

Water sluiced off Max's shoulders as he heaved himself out of the pool, turning to sit on the edge with his feet still in the water. This was his favorite time of day. Right as the sun came up and the world was quiet and new. No traffic sounds from below or the dull roar of speedboats on the bay. Just the morning birds and bugs.

He'd needed the solitude this morning. It gave him some time to process the gamut of emotions from the last couple of days. Yesterday went by in a whirlwind of preparation. Though he'd carved out some time to swim with the twins. And to put them to bed with Margot. But he hadn't given himself time—or permission—to think.

But in the water this morning, he'd given his mind free rein and sorted through the events of the last forty-eight hours. It took about twenty laps of the pool before it clicked that his entire life was about to change. His time as a bachelor, whether Margot was pregnant or not, was coming to an end.

And he was fine with that. He'd meant what he told her. For the right woman—her—he'd make the commitment.

As soon as he could, he planned to buy her a ring. He didn't want to wait another minute to make them a family.

A towel appeared next to his shoulder. He took it, words of thanks on the tip of his tongue, expecting to see Margot. But it was Tad.

Max frowned and wiped his face. "What are you doing up so early?"

Tad lifted a shoulder, slipping out of his sandals to sit down beside Max. His feet dropped into the water. "I don't sleep much. Never did. Came in really handy in med school."

Max gave a soft grunt of agreement, but otherwise stayed silent. He sensed Tad had something on his mind.

The man didn't make him wait long to find out what.

"Hey, um, I wanted to thank you." Tad cast him a quick look, then trained his gaze on the far side of the pool.

"For?"

"Watching out for Margot and the girls."

"I didn't do it for you."

"I know you didn't, but I still appreciate it. I'd be lying if I said I didn't worry about what would happen to them when I left."

Max clenched his teeth, anger simmering below the surface now. "Then why did you? Not that I'm complaining. Your loss is my gain." He knew it was a jerk thing to say, but Tad Gaultier didn't rate niceties after what he'd done.

Tad flinched. "I deserve that." He glanced away, staring off in the distance at the ocean visible over the jungle. "I left because I knew if I stayed, I'd just cause even more pain for them. Margot's strong. I knew she'd be okay. That she'd bounce back. And the girls were so young, I knew it would be unlikely they'd miss me for long." He paused, then turned to Max, self-deprecation twisting his face. "I didn't want my children to have the dad who was in prison. Who'd had everything and gambled it all away. Literally."

Max drew a knee up, wrapping his arms around it, and considered that. "Why'd you start gambling?"

"Do you know how expensive it is to raise a kid? I suddenly had two. Plus, my student loans from medical school." He shook his head, shrugging his shoulders. "I felt like I was drowning."

"Did Margot know how you felt?" She'd never mentioned any of this. But they hadn't talked too much about Tad and what went wrong.

Tad shook his head. "Not really. Not to that extent. She knew I was worried about the future. I brought up her inheritance once. Said we might need to tap into it as the girls aged. She shut that line of talk down quickly. Told me we'd find another way. I never understood why she was so adamant about not touching what her parents gave her."

"Did you bother to ask?"

"Of course I did." Indignation colored his voice and brought a slight glare to his face.

"Did you listen to what she said?" Because if he had, he'd know why she wanted nothing to do with it.

Tad huffed. "It would hurt her parents more to see her flaunt it in their faces."

Max wasn't so sure about that. From what Margot said of her parents, he doubted they'd even notice. And even if they did and took offense to her flaunting it, that wasn't Margot's style.

"It doesn't matter now. It's all water under the bridge." Tad filled his lungs, then slowly let the air out as he stared at the ocean again. "I know I screwed up." He looked at Max. "I won't stand in your way. Even if I thought she'd choose me over you, I'm in a lot of trouble. I left to keep her out of my mess and in a misguided attempt to protect them."

It was Max's turn to look out at the sea. "You know, I admire what you were trying to do." He held up a finger. "Not what you did or how you did it, but the sentiment behind it. But it's still fucked up. You should have sought help long before you got into the situation you did with Owens."

"Yeah." Tad's voice was soft. "Hindsight's twenty-twenty." He paused for a long moment. "Anyway, I just wanted to tell you that. And to say, please don't hurt them. They've been through enough." He turned to Max. "Maybe one day, tell my daughters I'm not a bad guy. Just misguided and royally stupid." Lifting a hand, it hovered above Max's shoulder for a moment. He let it drop in a brief touch before standing.

Max watched him scoop up his shoes and walk back to the house.

Heaviness settled into his heart. On the one hand, he was happy he was with Margot. That he had the chance to be Emily and Lily's dad. But on the other, he was sorry the girls would miss out on having Tad be the father Max now saw he could have been.

Thirty-Six

"Mommy, can we surfs?"

Margot looked up from the clinic build notes she was pouring over. It was so close to completion, but there were a million small details left. If all went to plan in the next few weeks or so, they'd open in early February.

Emily stood in front of her, dressed in her swimsuit. The top was on backward, but she didn't seem to care.

"Please, Mommy?"

Sighing, Margot set the papers down on the coffee table. "Em..." She wanted to say yes. It had been three days since they'd holed up at Max's. The first day hadn't been terribly difficult to keep the kids occupied. There was enough newness to it and enough people around to distract them. But yesterday, Em, especially, had wanted to leave the estate and go to the beach. Dean had created a monster.

"Please?" She put her little hands together and gave Margot puppy-dog eyes. "I need to pwactice."

A smile toyed with Margot's lips. She arched an eyebrow at her precocious daughter. "You do?"

Solemnly, she nodded. "So I can be a world champon."

"Oh, I see." She took Em's hands. "Remember how we talked about all the other people who are hanging around right now? How they're here to keep us safe?"

She nodded.

"I need to check with them and with Max to see if that's something we can do right now, all right?"

Expression falling, Em looked at the floor. "I wanna surfs," she muttered.

"And we will. It just might not be today." *Or tomorrow,* she silently added.

With a huff, Emily pulled away and stomped off. Margot picked up her phone to text Max.

She typed out a quick missive.

Where are you?

He and several of the others were keeping an eye on the grounds. Marchand, one of his colleagues, Sam, and Audra, had taken Tad into town—like the last couple of days—and were following him around inconspicuously while Tad pretended to keep an eye on Max's estate. They'd put out the word to Tad's contacts that he was looking for Berry and wanted to settle things, but so far, Berry hadn't shown his face. The hope was now that Berry would see Tad and make contact with him.

Dots appeared on her phone screen, then, *Walking the perimeter with Ford. What's up?*

Em wants to surf, she wrote back. *I'm not sure how long we can hold her off.*

He sent her an eye roll emoji, making her laugh. Dots appeared again.

Tell her we'll do an all-day trip, complete with a speedboat ride, once it's safe. And that she should put a boogie board on her Christmas list.

Margot's heart swelled. Her kids were so lucky to have him in their lives.

I'm sure she already has, but I will, she responded. *Be prepared to be pestered mercilessly.*

He sent a grinning emoji, then, *Eh, we'll play in the pool. I'll wear her out, and she'll forget all about it… until tomorrow.*

Smiling, Margot put her phone away and went in search of the girl.

When she walked into the back living room, Brooke looked up from her spot on the tile floor, where she played dolls with Lily.

"Hey." Brooke smiled. "Did Em find you? She said she had a question."

"She did. She wants to go surfing. I told her not today, but I messaged Max to tell him the natives were restless. He said to tell her he'd take her out for an all-day thing and a ride in the boat once it was safe." She frowned and glanced around. "Did she not come back here?"

"No."

Margot frowned, then remembered what Em had on when she appeared outside. "What was she wearing when she left you?"

It was Brooke's turn to frown. "The shorts and t-shirt you put her in this morning. Why?"

"Because she had her swimsuit on when she found me." Margot sighed. "Maybe she went back to her room to change. I'll go check. If she comes back in here or you spot her, text me?"

Brooke nodded. "Yep."

"Thanks." Spinning around, Margot started to head back the way she came, but decided to check the pool first. The girl had been wearing a swimsuit, after all. She doubted Em was there, it was fenced in, but Emily was as resourceful as they came. Margot wouldn't put it past her to find a way in.

Reaching the back of the house, she exited through the sliding doors and walked to the pool, peering in. It was empty.

Feeling more confident Em had gone to her room to change, Margot returned to the house and headed upstairs to the bedroom wing.

"Emily?" she called as she reached the landing.

Frustration built in Margot's gut when the girl didn't respond. She should have paid more attention to where she went. Em could hide in a corner and pout when she didn't get her way. At home, it wasn't too big of a deal. The house was small. But here, there were a lot of corners to hide in.

"Emily, honey, you need to tell me where you are. We don't play hide-and-seek in Max's house without rules on where you can hide, you know this." She pushed the girls' bedroom door open. The frilly pink and purple bedspreads were still in a heap, their pajamas laid on the end of the beds. Emily's outfit from earlier was on the floor by the dresser.

Sighing, Margot checked under the beds and in the closet. Em wasn't hiding in here.

Back in the hallway, she went into the next room, which was the one she'd been using. Even though the girls knew she and Max were in a relationship, Margot didn't want to move into his room until they were living in the house permanently. So, they'd stolen a few moments—or more—after the girls went to bed each night. There was enough upheaval in the kids' lives right now. They didn't need to worry about trekking further down the hall to find her if they awakened in the middle of the night. She'd like to move them down several rooms when they did eventually move in. Just so they were a little closer.

"Emily?" She knelt on the ground and peeked under the bed.

Nothing but dust bunnies.

With a huff, she sat up, frowning. Standing, she went to the closet.

It, too, was empty of a blonde-haired firecracker.

Spinning around, she marched into the hallway. "Emily! You need to come out now. I know you want to surf, but we can't today."

Margot continued into the next room, then the next, until she'd searched every bedroom on the floor. Getting more worried with each empty room, she hurried back downstairs to Brooke.

The woman looked up when Margot entered, her expression descending into a deep frown. "You didn't find her?"

"No."

Brooke stood, scooping Lily off the floor and onto her hip. "Come on, Lil. Let's help your mom look for Em."

They spread out. Margot went outside again, checking the pool once more. It was still empty.

And so was the bathhouse at the edge of the pool deck.

Hurrying back inside, Margot went into the kitchen. It was the ultimate hiding place for small children. She flung open cabinet after cabinet, looking inside, but there was no sign of her.

The frustration that had filled her until now descended into a touch of panic. Where was she?

Ten minutes later, with the entire house searched, Margot felt sick. She didn't know where she could have gone.

"Let's go check the cameras. Maybe they picked her up." Brooke tipped her head toward the panel on the wall.

"Do you have the access code to get to the stored footage?"

"No. Call Max."

Margot took out her phone and dialed.

He answered with a chuckle. "Is she still bugging you about it?"

"No. I can't find her. Brooke and I have checked the entire house and the pool. What's the code for the surveillance storage?"

He gave it to her without hesitation. "I'll be back in a few minutes to help you look."

When he hung up, Margot put her phone away and typed the code into the alarm system to access the stored footage. She backed it up to about the time Emily found her in the living room, then watched the doors.

About a minute later, Emily emerged from doors out of Max's office on the first floor. She still wore her swimsuit and no shoes. Moments later, she ran out of camera view toward the thick jungle. Margot's mouth flattened into a thin line. She hadn't missed Em by much when she stepped outside to check the pool.

"Where is she going?" Brooke muttered.

It hit Margot like a slap. She groaned, closing her eyes momentarily. "The beach." She looked at Brooke. "To surf."

THIRTY-SEVEN

Max burst through the tree line behind his house, Ford hot on his heels, and ran through the grass to the back door. Inside, Margot stood by the island, where Lily sat on a stool, eating a snack. Brooke was with her.

"What did you find? Anything?" he asked.

She looked at him, fear shining in her wide eyes. "She walked out your office door while I texted you earlier. We had the alarm off because we'd been in and out earlier and forgot to turn it back on." She swallowed hard. "It looks like she ran into the jungle." Her voice broke, and she slapped a hand over her mouth, a tear leaked out of her eye.

He closed the gap between them and gathered her into his arms. "We'll find her."

Ford laid a quick hand on Margot's shoulder, then walked around her. "I want to look at that footage. Get a bearing for which way she went."

She pushed out of Max's hold. "I think she left because I told her we couldn't surf. She wasn't very happy about that," she said, following him to the living room.

Max clenched his teeth. The beach wasn't that far. Just

down the hill and across the road. He took his phone from his pocket and called Sam.

"Go." Sam's one word greeting didn't surprise Max. They were all on alert for something to happen with Berry at any time.

"Emily ran away. We think she's headed down to the beach because she wants to surf."

"What? Are you serious?"

"Yes. Can you call the others—Marchand and crew included—and get them looking? She went down through the jungle at the back of the house. Opposite from where we were, of course. We're checking now to see if we can get a trajectory and figure out where she might come out."

"I'm on it. Call me back when you know." He hung up.

Ford stopped in front of the access panel for the surveillance system and keyed in the code to get to the stored footage.

Margot told him what time stamp to roll back to. In moments, Max watched the girl exit his office door, pause to look around, then dash toward the trees.

"That's what? Thirty degrees?" Ford glanced at him.

"About that, yeah," Max agreed.

Ford backed up. "All right. Let's go." He headed for the sliders on the rear living room wall.

At the door, Max paused to look at Margot. "You stay here."

"What?" A fierce, determined frown overtook her face. "No, I—"

"In case she comes home. I'll find her, honey. I promise." He leaned in and kissed her, then ran out the door behind Ford.

They hurried along the back side of the house to his office doors.

"How do you want to do this?" Ford asked.

"We go that way"—he pointed toward the jungle in the direction the girl ran—"and spread out maybe ten or twenty yards. Hopefully, she'll respond and not hide because she thinks she's in trouble."

"Let's go." Ford jogged away.

At the tree line, they split, plunging into the thick foliage.

"Emily!" Max called.

A few seconds later, he heard Ford call. He couldn't see him now. Max said a silent prayer they wouldn't walk right past her in the dense growth.

THIRTY-EIGHT

Adjusting his seat on the fallen tree he'd perched on, Tad Gaultier fanned himself with the fern frond he'd plucked from a nearby plant. He wished the marshals would have set him up in a car to watch Max's property. Then he'd have air conditioning blowing in his face. The Costa Rican jungle was stifling without a breeze blowing. And where he was sitting, there was little air movement.

The phone they'd given him buzzed in his pocket. Taking it out, he saw Marchand's number on the screen.

Tad sighed. He didn't want to talk to the marshal. Nothing new had happened since he called last. They should know that. They had eyes on him. But they still called to get an update on what he could see from his position.

He wanted to help. That's why he'd come here, why he'd agreed to this plan. The last thing he wanted was to put his family in danger. But it irked him that they wouldn't just let him sit here and stare at the driveway. What did they expect him to see? A car invisible to everyone except him?

"What?" he answered.

"I just got a call from Sam. One of your daughters took

off. Apparently, she doesn't like not being allowed to leave and go to the beach."

Tad's heart skipped, then started up double-time. "Jesus. It was Emily, wasn't it?"

"Yes. They have her on surveillance, leaving out one of the rear doors. She headed into the jungle and down the hill toward the beach. You're probably the closest of anyone. Start walking southeast along the road until you get to the side of the house. She'll have to cross to get to the water."

Immediately, Tad was on his feet. Leaving his cover, he jogged down the edge of the road.

"We've pulled everyone in to look for her. If you see her, call me back."

"Will do." Tad hung up. With both hands free now, he ran faster.

Nearing the side of the property, he slowed and looked up the hill through the trees.

How would they possibly find her in all that?

If she went in a straight line, she'd eventually come out to the road. But if she didn't, she could end up completely turned around and lost in the jungle.

From above, he could hear male voices shouting her name.

He added his to the mix.

"Emily!"

Jogging now, he scanned the trees. A curse slid past his lips as he stared at the dense foliage. It was like looking into quicksand. The jungle absorbed light. He couldn't see past a couple of feet.

With a quick glance up and down the road, he crossed the street and plunged into the trees, hoping that being immersed in it would help.

"Emily! Sweetie, it's—" He paused, swallowing back the word daddy. "It's Mommy's friend, Tad."

He stopped to listen, scanning the forest. When nothing

moved except some birds, he pushed in further, calling her name again.

Thirty feet up the hill, he glanced back at the road, which was now mostly out of view.

Maybe he should go back and watch the street, like Marchand said. The likelihood of him finding her was about as great as finding a needle in a haystack.

He turned around and started back down, glancing back and continuing to call her name.

A muffled, high-pitched shout of surprise stopped him in his tracks.

"Emily?"

Tad turned around again, running across and up toward the sound.

Rustling to his left drew his attention.

He saw a flash of blonde.

"Emily?" Hurrying over, he saw her sitting behind a log.

Relief flooded his veins, making him lightheaded. "Oh, thank God." Rounding the log, he squatted beside her. "Sweetie, are you all right? Why didn't you answer me?"

She looked up, a fierce pout on her face. "I wanted to surfs." She crossed her arms and glared.

Tad's eyes widened. She'd become far more independent and fearless in the time he'd been gone. He remembered her being strong-willed and a bit of a daredevil, but it still surprised him how determined she was to get to the beach.

"I heard. How about we go home and talk to your mom about it?"

"She said no."

He touched her knee, unable to help himself. "Did she give you a reason?"

"She said it's not safes."

"So, why did you go, then? Your mommy wouldn't lie to you."

"Daddy Max left. He'd stay if it wasn't safes."

Tad's heart clenched. He knew he'd screwed up, that it was his fault that he'd never hear the girls call him that again, but it still hurt.

"Come on." He stood up and held out a hand. "Let's get you home. Your mommy is very worried."

With a huff, she took his hand, knowing she'd lost her battle to get to the beach.

Tad glanced up the hill, then down, debating which way to go. It would probably be easier to go back to the road, then walk along the berm to the driveway, than to fight their way back up through the jungle.

Decision made, he scooped her into his arms, knowing it would be easier to carry her down the hill. She wasn't much taller than a lot of the vegetation.

"So, you wanted to surf, huh?"

She nodded.

"Whose surfboard were you going to use?"

"I use a boog-board."

"A boogie board?"

Again, she nodded.

"Ah, I see. Where did you plan to get one of those?"

"They has them at the beach."

"Oh. That makes sense, I guess." He said a silent prayer she hadn't made it down there. Tad had little doubt his resourceful daughter would find exactly what she wanted and go running into the ocean. He knew she could swim; he'd seen her. But swimming in the pool and swimming in the sea were two different things.

They emerged from the jungle, and he turned right. "I need to call the others. Let them know you're safe." Tad shifted her to his other side and reached into his pocket for his phone.

"Mommy's gonna be mad." Em's voice was soft, and she dipped her head.

"Maybe at first. Mostly, she'll be relieved you're safe." He dialed Marchand.

The sound of an engine revving had him glancing over his shoulder as the phone rang in his ear. A beat-up gray truck barreled toward them.

Tad stepped further off the road.

"Marchand."

The marshal's voice sounded in his ear, but Tad didn't respond. He couldn't. The face glaring at him through the windshield of the truck sent ice through his veins.

The pickup rocked to a halt just feet away, and the driver's door flew open.

Berry stepped out, a handgun clutched in his fist and pointed right at Tad. "Hang up the phone."

"Gaultier? Hey, you there?"

Marchand's voice quieted as Tad lowered the phone. He pretended to hang up, then shoved the device back in his pocket.

"There's no need for that, Fred. Put the gun away."

"Call it insurance. Get in the truck." Fred motioned to the passenger side.

"Let me take Emily back to her mother first."

"So you can sic her brute of a boyfriend on me? I don't think so." A mirthless smile flashed across his face. "Call the girl insurance too." As quickly as it appeared, the smile disappeared. "Get in."

Emily clutched Tad's neck. "He's a bad man."

"He is. But we need to do what he says for now, okay? I won't let him hurt you."

She hugged him a little tighter and nodded.

Tad walked forward, giving in to the only option he had. He got in the truck.

THIRTY-NINE

"Emily!"

Max's phone trilled as the echo of his voice faded, startling him. It wasn't Margot's ringtone, but one he used for miscellaneous callers.

Yanking the device from his pocket, he saw a number he didn't recognize.

"Carson," he answered.

"Berry's got Tad and the kid."

All the air froze in Max's lungs at Marchand's words. His knees wobbled, threatening to give out. *Dear God.* "What? You're sure?"

"Yes. Gaultier called me. But he never spoke directly to me. I heard him address Berry, then there was a bunch of muffled conversation, but I clearly heard him ask to take Emily back to her mom. I've sent Wurst and Beale down to his last known. Phillips is with me. I'm calling you from his phone. The call with Gaultier is still active. I can't hear much. I think he's sitting on it."

Heart thumping, Max's adrenaline spiked. That was good.

They could use that. "Text me the number for Tad's phone." He didn't wait for Marchand to respond, just hung up.

"Ford!" Max's bellow filled the jungle.

Heavy rustling came from his left. He didn't wait for his friend to arrive. Instead, he dialed Asher's number.

In seconds, Asher picked up. "Horn."

"I need you to track a phone. Berry took Tad and Emily."

Asher muttered a curse. "Okay. You got a number?"

Max pulled the phone back and checked his texts. "Marchand, you're amazing, thank you," he muttered. The man had sent the number without question. Louder, he read off the digits to Asher.

"I'm on it. Give me a couple minutes." The line went dead.

"Max? What's going on? Did you see her?" Ford came up beside him.

"No. Marchand called." Max turned, heading back up the hill. "Berry's got Tad. And Tad found Emily."

"Hell." Ford fell into step beside him. "You call Sam and Dean. I'll call Ezra and Edie."

As they ran, they made breathless phone calls, rallying the troops. Everyone was on their way by the time they broke through the trees into the backyard.

Max dashed across the grass to the sliding door to the living room. When he entered, he quickly scanned the space and saw Margot sitting on the couch, her head in her hands. Brooke sat beside her, running her hand over Margot's back. Lily was on her other side, clinging to her mother.

She looked up, and he knew Marchand had made contact by the bleak look in her eyes.

"We've got everyone coming." He hurried over and sank to his knees in front of her. "Marchand said the phone line is still active. He was on the phone with him when Berry took them.

Asher's already attempting to track the vehicle. There aren't many roads here. We'll find him."

She sniffed and nodded.

Max turned his attention to Lily, who stared up at him with her wide hazel eyes. "You doing okay, pumpkin?"

She nodded slightly, looking down. Her tiny fingers fiddled with the hem of Margot's shirt. "I miss Sissy."

"I know you do, honey. She'll be home soon."

The front door opened and Sam came through, Audra right behind him. They didn't even get to say hello before Max's phone rang again.

It was Asher.

"Go." Max put the line on speaker.

"They're at the marina."

Ford was quickly on his phone. He had an office there, still staffed at this time of day.

"I'll stay on it," Asher said. "Call me back if you need something else."

"Yep." Max hung up, then looked at Ford. "Well?"

He held up a finger, listening. A moment later, he responded to the person on the other end in Spanish, telling them to keep an eye on things, that they were on the way. He hung up. "They're boarding a boat. Let's go."

"You guys go ahead. Margot and I will take my car." They needed a car seat for Lily.

Ford nodded, already backing toward the door. "We'll see you there."

Max scooped Lily off the couch. "Time to go, honey."

"To get Sissy?" She wrapped her little arms around his neck, holding on as he headed toward the garage.

"Yep."

Dashing through the house, Max snagged the keys to his SUV off the wall by the garage, as well as the keys to all of his boats. He might need them.

"Get in," he told Margot. "I'll buckle Lily into her seat."

She ran around the side, climbing into the passenger seat as he deposited the girl into her seat and drew the belts over her shoulders. With her secured, he hopped into the driver's seat.

The engine roared to life with the push of a button. It was an agonizing few seconds as he waited for the garage door to open. Once it was up, he put the car in gear and pulled out, thankful he always backed in.

Heart pounding in his throat, threatening to choke him, he descended his driveway and turned onto the road. He had to force himself to swallow and to take a deep breath. Losing his shit wasn't an option. Not with Lily watching their every move.

So, he prayed. Harder than he ever had before. All the way to the marina, he prayed for Emily's safety as he clutched Margot's hand.

Finally, after what felt like eons, but was only a few minutes, he turned into the parking lot and brought them to a stop behind Ford's car.

"Where is everyone?" Margot scanned the area.

Ford and Sam's cars were empty. Max also spotted Dean's vehicle. "Not sure. In the office, maybe." He pulled on his door handle. "Let's go find out."

Margot climbed out, rounding the hood to meet him on the other side as he lifted Lily from her car seat. Together, they jogged toward Ford's office.

A sharp whistle from the water drew their attention. Max looked over to see Ford standing on one of his boats—the new one Brooke bought to replace the one that blew up last year—motioning to them. Brooke popped up from behind a pillar, a rope in her hands. She was on the dock, hurriedly untying lines.

"They took off!" Ford yelled.

Max ran toward the dock. "Not that boat. Mine's faster." He ran past Ford to where his speedboat was moored.

"It doesn't have the cover mine does," Ford called.

"Then follow me. I want to catch up, not wait for them to stop." Max came to an abrupt halt, though, considering Ford's logic. "Here." He passed Lily to Margot. "You two go with Ford. It's safer on his boat."

"Wha—" She took the girl. "Max!"

Feet thudded onto the dock, rattling it, as Sam, Audra, and Marchand jumped off Ford's boat.

"Go with Ford." He pointed as he backpedaled toward his vessel.

The three ran past Margot toward Max.

"Let's go!" Marchand yelled.

Giving Margot one last look, he waited long enough to see her nod, tears in her eyes, before he turned and followed them.

On board his speedboat, he found the right key and shoved it into the ignition. Sam pulled the lines and pushed them away from the dock.

"Ezra's going up in the bird. Edie and Jordan are too far away to get here before Ford casts off, so they're going to deal with the local police, along with Marchand's guys." Sam hooked a thumb toward the marshal. "Dean's on board with Ford. So are Brooke and Annabeth."

"Sounds good." Max eased the speedboat away from the slip and entered the harbor. He looked at Sam. "Did Ford say which way they went?"

"No. I—I don't know... if... Let me find out." Taking a deep breath, Sam raised his phone and dialed. A moment later, Spanish flowed from his mouth. He'd called the office and not Ford.

Max glanced back.

Sam nodded once, then pointed to the northwest. "That way. He said they were moving quickly too."

Easing the throttle forward, Max went as fast as he dared with the other boats around. If harbor patrol spotted him, they'd light him up for sure.

He didn't care. They could come along and help.

A minute later, they were away from the other vessels, and he opened up the throttle. "Hold on," he yelled.

The boat shot forward, and they were quickly cruising in open water.

Several minutes passed. Max glanced back, looking for Ford, but didn't see him. In the distance, he saw the dark shape of Ezra's chopper in the sky.

"There!" Marchand pointed ahead and to the right. "What's that?"

Max spun around, spotting a speeding boat in front of them. "Get the binoculars." He nodded toward the compartment below the dash, between the front seats.

Audra crouched beside him and rummaged inside, coming out with the specs. Sam held her steady while she aimed them at the white boat in the distance.

"It's them." She lowered the binoculars. "Tad's sitting on the bridge holding Em. Berry's driving."

"Did you see anyone else?" Sam asked.

"No."

Max glanced back, looking for Ford again. There were several boats behind them now, but he couldn't tell which one —if any—was Ford. He picked up the radio mic. "Ford, we've spotted them." He read the heading off his instruments.

"Copy. On your tail," came Ford's reply.

Satisfied they had backup on the way, Max focused on driving. The speedboat rapidly closed the gap with Berry's vessel, and soon, they were within a hundred yards.

He throttled back. "We need a plan. Are any of you armed?" He was betting they all were. He was and had been since the morning after they returned to Costa Rica.

Marchand lifted a hand. Sam and Audra shared a look, then they nodded.

A muffled crack sounded over the roar of the speedboat's engine. Water sprayed up just ahead as the round Berry shot hit the water.

They'd been noticed.

"If you get us closer, I can take a shot." Marchand moved forward to stand beside Max. "We're too far back, going too fast. I don't want to hit Gaultier or the girl."

Max ran the risks in his head. Yes, they were faster, but Berry had a better vantage point. The closer they got, the harder it would be to see him up on the bridge. They were also sitting ducks in this boat. It offered some cover if they crouched down, but not enough. He would need to do some fancy maneuvering.

"Everybody get down and hang on." Max hunched, hoping he was low enough, then opened the throttles up some again.

Swiftly, they closed the gap. More shots rang out, and he began weaving behind Berry's vessel.

"Pull up alongside him." Marchand duck-walked to the edge of the dash to Max's left.

Cutting hard to the right, Max throttled up further, bringing them along the boat's port side.

Gunshots pinged off the hull.

Marchand let out a yelp and fell back.

"He's been shot!" Sam crawled forward, pulling the marshal out of the open.

"How bad?" Max glanced back.

"I'll live." Marchand sat up. "But he hit my shooting arm."

Audra moved up to get the med kit from the same cabinet where she found the binoculars.

Anger roiled in Max's gut. They needed to get on board.

But not from this side.

He pulled back on the throttle and swung behind the boat, then sped up to come up along the other side.

"What are you doing?" Sam asked.

"Come up here."

A curious frown sat on Sam's face, but he didn't argue.

Max shifted to the side. "Take the wheel."

"What? Why? What are you planning?" He grabbed the wheel as Max let go.

"Get me as close to that boat as you can." Staying low, he walked around the dash.

"Max! You're insane. You'll never make it on board."

Maybe, but he wasn't going to let Berry get away with his little girl. "I've got a chance from this side. Get me closer."

Sam let out a frustrated growl but swung the boat toward Berry's.

The strip of water between the vessels disappeared. Max waited until they were practically touching before he stepped around the dash and climbed onto the starboard bow. Water sprayed him in the face, dampening his shirt. "Hold it steady!"

A bullet splintered the hull just feet away.

Max jumped.

Tucking himself into a ball, he hit the deck of Berry's boat and rolled. Coming up to his feet, he took two running steps toward the cabin and tucked himself against the wall, out of sight.

Above, he heard Emily scream, closely followed by a shout from Tad. A moment later, there was a heavy thud.

He needed a line of sight. But climbing the ladder to the bridge was out of the question. Berry would put a bullet through his skull before his shoulders cleared the floor.

Staying low, he hurried around the side of the boat, ignoring the railing and plastering himself to the windows. He'd come at him from the front. The angle would make it difficult for Berry to see him.

"He's got Em!" Sam yelled. "Tad's down!"

That made Max pause. Berry couldn't hold the girl, a gun, and steer.

He changed direction, deciding to chance the ladder. "Push him toward the right!" he yelled to Sam, swinging an arm and pointing. They needed to keep one of Berry's hands on the wheel.

Sam swung the speedboat away, then back at the other vessel at a sharp angle. Max grabbed the railing as the boat lurched to the right. A moment later, it swung left at the speedboat.

He climbed the ladder, hurtling himself into the pilothouse and drawing the handgun tucked into the holster at his back. In one quick glance, he took in the scene. Berry stood at the wheel, Em tucked under his arm, the gun on the dash within reach. Tad was on his forearms and knees, head hanging. Blood dripped from his temple near his hairline onto the floor. He was awake, but appeared dazed.

Max leveled his weapon on Berry. "Stop the boat!"

"Daddy Max!" Emily squirmed in the man's hold.

Berry let go of the wheel and picked up the pistol on the dash, holding it to Emily's side.

"Back off! I'll shoot her!"

Max took one hand off his gun, holding it up. "You don't want to do that. You shoot her, and you're dead. Simple as that." He took a step closer. "Give me the girl."

"Stay back!"

The whites of Berry's eyes shone bright in the sunlight.

Max planted his feet. He wanted to rush him, but the man was on the brink. He had nothing to lose.

Tad lifted his head. Fury had turned his hazel eyes to a flinty steel.

Oh yeah. Max's inner voice fist-pumped. Tad wasn't as hurt as he appeared. He was playing possum.

He met Tad's gaze, letting him know he knew.

"Let me go!" Emily pushed against Berry's hold.

"Em, it's okay. Just hold still," Max reassured her. He didn't want her to get shot accidentally because she moved the wrong way.

But, in typical Em fashion, she ignored him. Like some sort of contortionist, she turned her upper body, wrapping her hands in the collar of Berry's shirt. Using it as leverage, she raised herself high and leaned in. Her little teeth clamped down on his ear.

Berry let out a howl. The gun moved away from Em's side, and Max pounced.

He took two running steps and was on the man, grabbing his gun hand and keeping it aimed at the floor. A shot went off, going through the deck.

Tad pushed to his feet. Hands appeared in Max's field of vision, plucking Emily from Berry's grasp.

With the girl out of the way, and not wanting to risk another shot going wild, Max palmed his pistol and aimed an open-handed punch at Berry's face, striking him in the nose.

"Ugh!" Berry's head whipped back and bright red blood spurted from his nostrils.

Max yanked on the man's shooting arm, twisting it and putting pressure on the nerve that would make him drop the weapon. His hand opened, and the gun fell to the floor with a clatter. Pushing forward, he shoved Berry into the dash, pulling his arm up until his fingers were between his shoulder blades.

"Ow! Fuck, let go!"

"No. Don't move." Max leaned in, holding him there. He glanced at Tad. "Are you all right? Is Em?"

Tad sat against the far wall of the pilothouse, clutching Emily to his chest. He was bloodied, but alert, and she appeared to be fine.

"We're okay." A lopsided smile formed on his face. "Fred, you picked the wrong twin to mess with."

Max chuckled. That was the truth. He motioned Tad over with a quick tip of his head. "Come slow us down."

Tad got up, still holding Emily.

As he neared and reached for the throttle, Em tipped herself in his arms so she could look into Berry's face. "You is a bad man."

Berry groaned and closed his eyes.

Max laughed. "I'm gonna make sure it gets around your prison group that you got taken down by a two-year-old."

The man groaned again.

As the boat slowed, Max took a deep breath. Relief made his hands shake.

It was over.

FORTY

Margot's heart pounded in her chest as Ford slowed, coming up behind the two boats. Max had already radioed them that Berry was in custody, but she wouldn't relax until she had her baby in her arms.

Sam tossed several bumpers over the side of the charter boat as Ford came up alongside. Brooke threw him a rope, and they lashed the vessels together.

Once they were secure, Margot scrambled onto the bench seat on the deck and climbed over the side onto the other boat. Her feet hit the deck, then she was up the ladder and into the pilothouse.

"Emily!"

"Mommy!"

Em leaned out of Tad's arms toward her. She took the girl and clutched her tight.

"Oh!" She buried her face in Em's silky hair, breathing in her scent. "I'm so glad you're safe."

"I'm sorry, Mommy. I forgots about the bad man. I just wanted to surfs." The little girl's eyes watered.

"I know, honey. It's all right. You're safe. But no more

running off, okay?" She squeezed her tight before pulling back.

Expression solemn, Emily nodded.

"She's one-hundred-percent fine." Max stepped over, running a hand down Emily's hair. "She even helped save herself."

"I bited the bad man."

"She did," Max affirmed. "On the ear."

Margot's heart flip-flopped again at the thought of her daughter putting herself in danger. She wasn't really surprised, though. The child was a complete daredevil.

"Emmy!"

Margot looked up to see Lily waving from Ford's boat.

"Come on. Let's get on Ford's boat. Your sister missed you too."

"I'll help you down," Tad said. He paused and glanced at Max. "If you don't mind?"

"Not at all." He gave Em a quick kiss on the top of her head, then looked at Margot. "I'll see you soon, okay?"

She nodded, glancing past him at a bloodied and tied up Berry, anger surging for what he'd done. Only the fact that the twins could see her kept her from walking over and delivering a swift kick to his face.

But it was over, and he wouldn't see the light of day for a long, long time. Exactly what he deserved. Yelling at or hurting him wouldn't change anything. So, she spun around and headed down the ladder.

Sam and Dean helped her and Tad over the railings onto Ford's boat. She took Emily inside the cabin and set her on the couch. Annabeth brought Lily, and the girls gave each other a quick hug.

"I missed you, Emmy. You done a bad thing. Mommy cried."

Emily's lower lip wobbled. She looked at Margot. "I's sorry, Mommy."

Margot leaned in and kissed the girl's forehead. "It's over now." They'd talk about consequences later. Once they'd all calmed down more. Most likely, that would be no surfing or bodyboarding for a period of time.

As she straightened, she caught a glimpse of Tad standing to the side. Blood coating his somber face, he watched them.

"You two stay here for a minute, all right? I need to help your—to help Tad get cleaned up." He had a nasty gash on his temple that was oozing blood.

Emily nodded, then turned, glancing out the window. "Ohhh, it's the bad man." She nudged her sister and pointed. Lily scrambled up to her knees, and they both perched on the seat to stare through the window at the hive of activity going on outside. Margot could see Dean climbing aboard the other boat, a large first-aid kit in his hands.

"I better go help him." Annabeth backed toward the door.

Margot nodded. "Thank you for staying with Lily."

"Anytime." With a smile and a quick wave, she left.

She was glad Annabeth was the one tending to Berry's bloody face. If it had been her, she might have done her best to make it worse, Hippocratic Oath be damned.

"I'll be right back, girls."

"Okay, Mommy," Lily said, her eyes on the sky.

Above, Ezra circled in the chopper. Margot doubted he'd stay long. There wasn't much he could do from the air now.

Crossing the small cabin, she dug into the cabinet in the galley where she knew Ford kept emergency supplies. Finding the bag, she turned to Tad. "Come over here and let me look at your head."

"It's fine. Nothing a few butterfly strips won't fix."

"Humor me." She pointed at the small banquette built into the wall. "Sit."

He huffed, but did as she asked.

Margot set the bag on the table and unzipped it. The contents crinkled and knocked together with a dull clack. Cellophane rustled as she found a syringe of sterile saline. Popping it out of its wrapper, she picked up a gauze packet and ripped it open, then dampened it with the saline.

"Tilt your head." She brushed his hair back, then wiped at his face with the wet gauze. "How did this happen?"

"He hit me with the gun. Luckily, it was just a glancing blow." His jaw worked. "It was enough, though. He took Em from me."

"Don't blame yourself for that. Especially since you kept her safe. Marshal Phillips told me what Marchand overheard. How you tried to get her back to me. And we wouldn't have known he'd taken you onto a boat if you hadn't kept the line open. That was brilliant." She tossed the bloody gauze onto the table and picked up another square, wetting it.

"Still. She wouldn't even have been in danger if I hadn't brought it to her." He grimaced, but not from her ministrations. "This is why I left. To keep all of you safe."

That old anger she thought she'd long buried over him leaving reared its head. She swiped at his wound a little harder than she should have, and he hissed.

"Sorry," she muttered. Swallowing down all the pain and fury from back then, she looked at him through her lashes. "I wish you'd come to me. Before you sold your soul to Owens."

"So do I. But I... I couldn't. I was so ashamed of what I'd already done. I didn't want to see you look at me with disappointment in your eyes. I knew then that you and the girls deserved better than me. Someone more like Max."

Margot sucked in a breath. "What we deserved was to not be lied to." She stopped and turned his head so she could look him in the eye. "I thought you were dead."

He dropped his gaze.

She barreled ahead. "Instead, you went into hiding and other people died."

He stiffened, pulling his face from her grip. "I regret that."

"I'm sure you do." She reached into the first-aid kit again and found the butterfly strips. "Especially since I'm sure the FBI will prove you had something to do with Dale Conroy's death."

Tad stayed silent, only confirming her suspicions. Margot's gut churned. She hadn't wanted to believe he was capable of murder, but it seemed like she'd been wrong.

"I didn't do it on purpose," he said, his voice soft. "What happened with Conroy... it was an accident. He got greedy. We argued." His jaw worked. "That was that."

She held up a hand. "Don't say anymore. I don't want to be obligated to testify against you."

He fell silent. Margot found an antibiotic ointment packet and squeezed some onto the cut, then tore open the butterfly strips and applied them to the wound. Once that was done, she put a square of gauze over the top and taped it in place.

Stepping back, she gathered her trash. "There you go."

"Thanks." He stood up, fingering the edge of the bandage.

"You're welcome." She turned, heading for the trash can.

"Margot."

She paused, glancing back.

"For what it's worth, I'm sorry. For everything. Then, and now. I know it doesn't change anything. I just—" He stopped, his face scrunching with a frown.

"I know, Tad." Some of her anger faded, replaced by a bone-deep sorrow. She didn't regret where life had taken her; she loved Max and wanted to be with him. But she mourned for what she'd had, and she mourned for what the man she'd once loved had lost.

Retracing her steps, she laid a hand on his forearm. "Why don't you spend a little time with the kids before Marchand takes you into custody? I still think it's best they don't know who you really are right now. But one day, we can fix that. When they're old enough to comprehend all that's happened."

He glanced at the twins, whose gazes were still transfixed on the world outside, then nodded. "Will you write to me? Keep me updated on how they're doing? And send me pictures? Maybe let me wish them happy birthday and Merry Christmas?" He held up a hand. "As a friend."

A soft smile flitted over her face. "I think that would be fine. I'm sure Emily will want to know how her rescuer is doing."

Tad turned to look at Em, a genuine smile crinkling the corners of his eyes. "She's something else. They both are." He sobered slightly. "You've done such a great job with them."

"I had help. Annabeth was a godsend. And then all of Dean's friends. Life is not what I ever imagined it would be, but I'm happy. And so are they." She tipped her head toward Em and Lily.

He covered her hand. "I'm glad." Looking down, he lightly ran his thumb over her knuckles. "Again, I'm sorry for all I've done and the way I left. This time, I'll say goodbye before I go."

She smiled. "At least this time, we'll know it's just goodbye for now."

His mouth tipped up. "Yeah. And that's much better than I ever thought I'd get."

FORTY-ONE

N*ine days later...*

The delighted shrieks of the twins' laughter filled Max's living room as they played with their Christmas presents. He sat on the couch, sipping a mug of steaming coffee while he watched them drive their remote-controlled unicorns in bumper cars around the floor. They'd rammed most of the furniture in the beginning, but it hadn't taken long for them to get the hang of the controls. Now, they zoomed in and out of table legs and around chairs, racing each other to an imaginary finish line.

Margot sank onto the cushion beside him and propped her chin on his shoulder. "Those are brilliant. Where did you find them?"

"Online. Actually, Esther found them. I'd mentioned wanting to get the girls something interactive when I talked to Asher last week. She overheard and started googling. I swear, her research skills rival his."

Margot chuckled. "It makes them a good match."

"It does. Anyway, she found those, and I could hear her laughter from across the room. She showed them to Asher first and all he said was, 'Christ almighty.' She didn't even need to tell me what they were after that. I knew they'd be perfect."

"He's never going to live down the unicorn thing."

"Nope. Especially since the things he crafted from that suit probably would have saved his life if events hadn't happened the way they did."

She hummed. "Speaking of perfect gifts... here." She brought a small box around, holding it in front of him.

Curiosity drew his eyebrows together. "You already gave me presents."

"I know. But this one is extra special."

Max took the box and glanced at her. Anticipation shone in her eyes. "Okay?" He gave it a shake. The box was light, but it didn't make any noise.

Margot rolled her eyes. "Don't try to guess. Just open it."

Chuckling, he pulled the bow off. "Every day, I swear, I'm reminded where Em gets her impulsivity and impatience."

"I won't deny that," she said with a chuckle.

Still smiling, he lifted the lid.

His entire body stilled, and the smile fell off his face. Eyes growing round, his gaze darted to hers, then back to the box. With shaking fingers, he lifted the white strips from the tissue paper. "Are—are these what I think they are?"

A beautiful, radiant smile spread over her face. "Yes. In probably early September, we'll be a family of five."

Heart thumping so hard it rattled his ribs, Max stared at the two pink lines on the test strips. He'd hoped for this. They'd done little to stop it from happening. But there had still been a piece of him that doubted it would happen. Especially so quickly.

He dropped the box into his lap and framed her face between his hands to press a swift kiss to her lips. When he pulled back, happiness bubbled out on rich laughter. "Oh my God! If it never happened, I'd have been ecstatic just to be a dad to Em and Lily. This is just icing on the cake." He kissed her again. "I love you, woman."

Still beaming, she laid her hands over his, holding his gaze. "I love you too."

After another quick, fierce kiss, he let her go. She wasn't the only one with an unexpected gift.

Shifting on the couch, he buried a hand in his pocket.

"What are you doing?" Margot gave him a curious frown.

"I've been carrying this around for close to a week, trying to find the right time to give it to you. Now seems like a great time." Pulling his hand out, he opened his palm, revealing the delicate diamond and pearl ring.

She gasped.

"The pearls are for the girls. It's their birthstone. I'm not just committing to you. I know you're a package deal, and I wanted to honor that."

"Oh, Max." She let her hand fall. "It's beautiful."

"Will you marry me, Margot?"

The little squeal she let out and the ear-to-ear grin were the only warnings he received before she launched herself at him, wrapping her arms around his neck. He curled his fist around the ring and held her close.

"Is that a yes?" he asked with a soft laugh.

She cradled his face. "What do you think?"

He grinned. "Well, I think a New Year's Eve wedding sounds amazing."

"Me too."

The next instant, she melded their mouths together in a kiss that curled his toes.

With a soft moan, he eased back. "You should probably put this on before I forget it's in my hand and we end up tearing the couch apart to find it." He opened his hand, showing her the ring.

Laughing, she held up her fingers.

Max slipped it over her knuckle, then kissed the back of her hand. "Thank you for showing me that anything is possible. Even dreams I thought were long dead."

"I think we showed that to each other." Leaning forward, she nestled against his chest.

He wrapped an arm around her, content to hold her as the girls ran around, still racing their cars.

This was better than his dream had ever been.

Thank you for reading *Max's Mission*! I hope you loved it! This marks the end of the *Wagner Brigade* series. I'm sad to say goodbye to the characters, but excited to begin a whole new world soon. Just in case you missed it, you can stay with our Wagner Brigade friends a little longer and read about Ezra. He has his own book! *Stranded With Ezra* is available an Amazon: https://books2read.com/u/mBAX9M.

If you'd like to read more about Max & Margot (and the other characters in this series), join my mailing list. Subscribers get a bonus chapter or scene after every book! You'll also get access to exclusive teasers, giveaways, and the occasional book recommendation, as well as sneak peeks into my world as I create my stories. Scan the QR code below to sign up and get your bonus scene!

bitly

About the Author

Ashley started writing in her teens and never stopped. Her first novel, Smoky Mountain Murder, came out in 2016, and she has since published two more series and has plans for more. When not writing, you can find her with her nose stuck in a book or watching some terrible disaster movie on SyFy. An avid baseball fan, she also enjoys crafting and cooking. She lives in Ohio with her husband, two kids, three cats, and one very wild shepherd mix.

Website: https://ashleyaquinn.com
Facebook Reader Group: facebook.com/groups/349932159616427

goodreads.com/ashleyaquinn

amazon.com/Ashley-A-Quinn/e/B07HCT4QST

facebook.com/ashleyaquinn.writer

instagram.com/ashleyaquinn.writer

ALSO BY ASHLEY A QUINN

The Broken Bow

A Beautiful End

Wildfire

In Plain Sight

Close Quarters

Scorched

Light of Dawn

Pine Ridge

Sweetness

Loner

Shark

Katydid

Homespun

Foggy Mountain Intrigue

Smoky Mountain Murder

Smoky Mountain Baby

Smoky Mountain Stalker

Smoky Mountain Doctor

Smoky Mountain K-9

Smoky Mountain Judge

Prequel to Wagner Brigade

Stranded with Ezra

Wagner Brigade

Ford's Fight

Dean's Dilemma

Jordan's Journey

Sam's Salvation

Asher's Assignment

Max's Mission

www.ingramcontent.com/pod-product-compliance
Lightning Source LLC
Chambersburg PA
CBHW061345310726
48974CB00001B/204